Praise for *The Gospel According to Billy the Kid*

"In this breezy, alternative history of the Lincoln County War and the outlaw we know as William H. Bonney, first-time author Dennis McCarthy has fun with the counterfactual claims of Brushy Bill Roberts in 1950. It's a fast, entertaining read."

—RON HANSEN, author of *The Kid* and *The Assassination of Jesse James by the Coward Robert Ford*

"Just when you think you've read everything that could be written about Billy the Kid, Dennis McCarthy has come up with an engaging, inventive, and unique take on the outlaw legend. Sit back, smile, and enjoy the ride."

—JOHNNY D. BOGGS, author of *Return to Red River*

"Both propulsive and poignant, McCarthy's fresh take on the Billy the Kid legend is both a compelling tale of the old West and an engaging study of one of its most enduring characters."

—C. JOSEPH GREAVES, author of *Hard Twisted: A Novel*

"*The Gospel According to Billy the Kid* has the pace of a mountain river, moving with a similar power and inevitably toward its destination, yet like a mountain river, Dennis McCarthy's novel has depths that lead us toward profound questions of culpability, forgiveness, and grace, and what realms may lie beyond this world. This novel does what all of the best ones do: we enter them, but they also enter us, and they stay."

—RON RASH, author of *In the Valley* and *Serena: A Novel*

The Gospel According to Billy the Kid

The Gospel According to Billy the Kid

A Novel

Dennis McCarthy

University of New Mexico Press | Albuquerque

 Published 2021
Printed in the United States of America

ISBN 978-0-8263-6235-3 (paper)
ISBN 978-0-8263-6236-0 (electronic)

Library of Congress Cataloging-in-Publication data is on file with the Library of Congress.

Cover illustration: adapted from photograph by Ben Wittick, ca. 1879
Designed by Felicia Cedillos
Composed in Adobe Garamond Pro 12.25/14.25

To my beloved Judy and
my friend and mentor Peter Josyph,
my most dedicated readers

Doubts of all things earthly, and intuitions of some things heavenly;
this combination makes neither believer nor infidel,
but makes a man who regards them both with equal eye.

—HERMAN MELVILLE, *Moby-Dick*

Acknowledgments

This book is a work of fiction. Like Pat Garrett's *The Authentic Life of Billy the Kid* it is largely a product of the author's imagination. Some of the episodes are based on fact, just as the stories in *The Authentic Life* are based on fact. Eyewitnesses to the historic events, however, told different versions of what they saw, and records that historians might reasonably rely upon are sketchy at best. While we know a fair amount about the Lincoln County War, which provided the background for the rise and fall of Billy the Kid, we know very little about Billy himself. We don't know where or when he was born. We don't know for certain when he died. We don't even know his real name.

The Gospel According to Billy the Kid is my first novel. As it turned out, I needed help. I sent different drafts to various friends along the way. And there were many drafts. I lost count a long time ago. My wife Judy read the first draft. Judy has always been my first editor throughout my personal and professional life. Gratefully, Judy was kind and tolerant and she gave me incentive to forge ahead.

Deborah Scaperoth read an early draft and helped with structural problems. Readers of later drafts provided encouragement and corrected gaffes and inaccuracies or recommended deleting sections that people will skip anyway. Some pointed out lacunae or suggested topics that clarified the text or made images more vivid. Tom Poland told me that rattlesnakes smell like burnt sugar, and Allen Josephs corrected Billy's Spanish. My editor at the University of New Mexico Press,

Stephen Hull, took a chance on an unknown author and gave me valuable guidance in bringing the book to press.

To all of them I am indebted: Terry Chilcoat, Angie Corbett-Kuiper, Steve Davis, Mike Evans, Paulo Faria, Laurence Gonzales, Chuck Grieves, Stephen Hull, Jon Jefferson, Allen Josephs, Peter Josyph, Brother Leander, Cormac McCarthy, Judy McCarthy, Desley Pendergast, Tom Poland, Deborah Scaperoth, Greg Tinsley, and Amanda Urban. There was a long gestation period for this project, and I've undoubtedly left out some readers. I apologize to them. If I'd written this story thirty years earlier I wouldn't have been so forgetful.

Of all my readers the one to whom I owe the greatest debt is Peter Josyph. Peter goaded me into the project, encouraged me throughout, was my second most merciless editor, right after my brother Cormac, and taught me the most. Thanks, pal.

PROLOGUE **August 1914**

Cowboys are good-hearted and kind, sympathetic and not looking for trouble if it can be avoided, but nevertheless, when nothing but trouble will do, you have struck the right party when you strike the average cowboy.

—JAMES EMMIT MCCAULEY, *A Stove-Up Cowboy's Story*

YOU DON'T REMEMBER ME, DO you? The San Carlos Reservation? We both had more hair back then. You were scouting for the army. I'd quit a job at Fort Grant and was headed to the White Mountains. We went hunting together along the Gila, and you shot the biggest mule deer I've ever seen. We were hauling it back to San Carlos when we ran into Gerónimo. He'd run off the reservation with a bunch of his boys. I was glad you spoke Apache.

I've thought a lot about you since. Mostly because of your brother Carlos. He saved my life. Wasn't for him I wouldn't be here. I'd be buried back of some Mexican whorehouse, my throat cut. Or gutshot stealing cattle. Or bushwhacked on the Spanish Trail and carried off by coyotes.

I've knowed scores of fine men over the years but none like Carlos. He was extraordinary. Most likely you don't remember him much. You were pretty young when he left home.

I'm glad I finally ran into you again. Wasn't sure I ever would. I found your brother's diary after he died and I've been carrying it around ever since. It's unusual for a diary. He talks more about what he thought than what he did. I've read it probably a dozen times. Believe he'd want you to have it.

Like to tell you about your brother. What I knew anyway. Don't know where to begin except at the beginning, before I met Carlos. It'll help you understand why he means so much to me. It started with the Lincoln County War. Might take most of the afternoon. If you're up to it, whiskey's on me.

Hear tell I was famous but I don't know that ole boy. He's a product of Pat Garrett's imagination. Him and Ash Upson. They say I killed twenty-one men? Not if they're talking about hombres I knew. It was five. I've shot at others but don't know if I hit any. If you want to include Comanches and Spaniards during wartime, I may of killed twenty-one. I'm a fair shot and hombres fell when I pulled the trigger, but I wasn't the only fool shooting. Ain't no claiming credit for killing in war anyway.

I ain't proud of killing the ones I knew. At the time I told myself they deserved it, or they didn't give me no choice. I've learned to live with most of it. The first one though was my own doing. Joe Grant. I was a banty rooster and he tried to clip my spurs. We were in Bob Hargrove's saloon in Fort Sumner. We'd been drinking. Joe more'n me. He bet me a double eagle he'd kill a man before I did. I already had a reputation. Folks'd heard stories. Like one about me killing a blacksmith in Fort Grant. Wasn't true but I never denied it. I knew what Joe was thinking. Considered ignoring him, but Joe was a bad drunk. I should of walked away. Would of today.

I was working on the Chisum ranch on the Pecos. Me and two of Chisum's Jinglebob hands were at the bar when Joe challenged me to the bet. Then he lifted an ivory-handle six-shooter from the holster of one of the hands and replaced it with his own Colt with wooden grips. The cowboy was savvy enough to let it slide, but I was a sucker for the challenge. I reached over and lifted the six-shooter from Joe's holster.

"Nice pistol you got there, Joe," I said as I twirled it on my finger. "Bit fancy though, even for you."

I spun the cylinder and handed it back. He slapped it in his holster. I turned and walked away.

What Joe didn't know was that the cowboy'd fired twice at a jackrabbit coming into Fort Sumner. He hadn't reloaded. When I spun the cylinder I made sure the next shot'd land on an empty case.

"Fancy pissant ain't ye," Joe said to my back.

When I heard the hammer snap I spun round and ripped three shots into Joe's chin. He fell backward, dropping the six-shooter. I picked it up and handed it to its owner.

Joe was right. I was a pissant. I baited him into drawing. Never done that before or since. It still bothers me.

Not the three shots though. You could of covered them with the double eagle I never collected.

I was an outlaw. Not a bandido, just an outlaw. No more'n most men. It was hard not to be an outlaw back in them days. You know how it was. Wasn't much alternative. No real law. The governor, sheriff, politicians—all of them crooks. The rest of us were shoestringers, trying to take back what the bigwigs stole from us. It says somewhere we hang the small thieves and appoint the big ones to office. Sounds about right.

My boss John Tunstall wasn't no outlaw. His lawyer Mac McSween might of been but I doubt it. The Lincoln County War started when Mac didn't divvy up a dead man's insurance money the way some folks thought he should. They say Mac stole the money. I don't know. He seemed too God-fearing for a thief. Lots of God-fearing men are thieves but Mac's religion was real. I doubt anyone but Mac knew for sure. Maybe not even him. His wife Sue might of knowed. She once said that when her and Mac left Kansas, headed out here, Mac owed some hombre three hundred dollars that he never paid.

So here's the gospel story. Gospel as I know it anyway. Memory's a funny thing. It'll fool you. One of my early memories was seeing my pa coming home to Buffalo Gap with Quantrill after a raid in Kansas. I can see the two of them now coming through the high grass, as clear as I'm standing there. Pap rode with Quantrill alright, but he never brought him to Buffalo Gap. That don't change my memory none.

Buffalo Gap's where I come from. It's in Taylor County now. Was just Texas back then.

The things I'm gonna tell you happened thirty, thirty-five years ago. I ain't sure about dates. To most folks back then—especially farmers and ranchers—seasons were important. Today, tomorrow, and next week were important, but only for a few days. Folks didn't pay much mind to dates. Lots of folks didn't know how old they were. I ain't sure myself.

My story begins on February 18, 1878. You're probably wondering how I remember that date. It's one I don't aim to forget. It's the day John Tunstall died.

CHAPTER I **The Río Feliz Ranch**

He is, in all, quite a handsome fellow, the only imperfection being two prominent front teeth slightly protruding like squirrels' teeth, and he has agreeable and winning ways.

—*The Santa Fe Gazette*, DECEMBER 1880

"HEY, BISCUIT BOY. GET YOUR butt out of bed."

Dick Brewer kicked my bunk.

"Gauss ain't here. You're doing breakfast. We've got work to do. John wants us and Rob to run the horses and mules to my ranch, then head to Lincoln for supplies. Rob's rounding up the stock."

"Ain't nobody built a fire in this barn?" I said, pulling a quilt over my head.

My cot was in a corner of the bunkhouse furthest from the fireplace. The bunkhouse was a dirt-floor jacal. The chimney was the only clue that chickens didn't live there. The last cowhand had banked the fire before bedding down for the night. By morning only a few coals remained. The cup of coffee beside my cot was rock solid. The sun was up but hardly any light seeped through the shuttered windows. Of course the cold had no problem. It could seep through the windows and door and walls too. When it snowed, flakes rode in on the wind.

"The quicker you shed that bedroll the quicker your blood'll flow," Dick said. "Me and Rob's done half a day's work while you've been dreaming about your girl. How you lay in bed after first light's a mystery to me."

"Ain't my girl," I said. "Been dreaming about Aunt Cat. She was wearing a long dress, like a wedding gown, only it was black. She was holding a dead raven by its feet. You think dreams mean something?"

"I think your aunt's telling you that if you don't get your sorry ass out of bed, Billy Bonney, you'll be crow meat for John."

Billy Bonney's the name I was using back then. Aunt Cat was born in Belfast. She raised me after my folks was killed by Comanches. She called me her bonny Billy. I flipped the name around. I was the youngest of John Tunstall's hands. Except for John's old cook, Dad Gauss, the hands weren't much more than boys. Henry Brown was a year or two older than me. The rest—Fred Waite, John Middleton, Rob Widenmann, Dick Brewer—were in their twenties. John too.

Fred was my closest friend among the hands. He was part Chickasaw. He grew up in Indian Territory. He was smart and had a college education. After the Lincoln ruckus he went back to Indian Territory and became attorney general of the Chickasaw Nation. I reckon he's still there. I ran into him once in Oklahoma City when I was in Buffalo Bill's Wild West Show. He'd looked me up.

Money was Henry Brown's undoing. He'd worked for Lawrence Murphy for a year before going to work for John. He quit Murphy because he never got paid. Then when John got killed, he lost his wages again. Eventually he became a marshal in Medicine Lodge, Kansas. I reckon marshaling didn't pay much neither because he robbed the local bank. Got caught trying to get out of town. A lynch mob killed him the next day.

Don't know for sure what happened to Middleton. He took a bullet at Blazer's Mill and nearly died. I'll tell you about that in a moment. He drifted away afterward. I heard he died of smallpox near Silver City a few years later, but Fred said he drowned in Kansas about the time Henry was killed.

Rob Widenmann was a strange bird. A blowhard and a liar, but folks liked him. John made him administrator of his estate. When John got killed, Rob thought being administrator meant he got the ranch. He met a peculiar end. I'll tell you about that later too. It's quite a story.

Dick Brewer was the best of us. He was John's foreman. A hard worker with a good heart. He had a girl back East. After he bought a ranch on the Ruidoso he asked her to come live with him. He bought a load of pecan wood from Texas and built her a bed. A rattler bit her soon after she arrived and she died in that bed. Dick took it apart and made a coffin of it. He buried her out back where he could watch over her from the bedroom window. I'll tell you about his undoing when I get to Blazer's MIll.

John Tunstall, our boss, was an Englishman, born in London a few years before the War between the States. His family was rich. They owned mercantiles in London and British Columbia. John'd worked in the British Columbia store. I believe it was in Victoria. Something happened. John could of been the cause. I got the impression his pa was looking to him to restore whatever the family lost. That's why he came to Lincoln and bought the ranch on the Río Feliz. He saw a new country brimming with promise.

When John got to Lincoln he met Mac McSween. They were both smart, well educated, quick to be compadres. They opened a store together in Lincoln. Mac was a lawyer. He kept an office in the store.

John was different from us hands. He was different from anyone I ever knew. He was blind in one eye and looked at you cockeyed. Talked like he had a spoke up his ass. He wore English riding britches that stuck out on the sides like wings. He had the prettiest Arabian bay you ever saw. When he sat that bay with his hand-tooled English saddle, hand-tooled riding boots, winged britches, cutaway coat, he was a sight. He was great to work for. Treated me like a brother. One of the best men I ever knew.

John had near four thousand acres on the head of the Río Feliz and four hundred head of cattle. He lived in a stone choza a chicken run from the bunkhouse. Wasn't much. Three rooms strung in a line. He slept in one end of the house. The kitchen was in the other. He planned to build a ranch house but Dolan's boys squashed that idea.

The ranch was mostly hill country with barely enough grama to starve a lazy cow. The hills were peppered with piñons and junipers. Cottonwoods lined the Feliz. It was hardly a river. You could walk across it in places without getting your boots wet. It ran a couple of miles through the draws before leaving the ranch. Mostly, the ranch needed water. Hadn't rained since late summer and folks said the winter snow was the poorest in memory.

The hands ate in John's house. I was cook whenever Gauss was gone. I'd learned to cook in a grub house outside Fort Grant. That was before I met you on the San Carlos. The boys groused and groaned if I was cooking, but I put out a good feed and they knew it.

That morning I dragged out of bed in my long johns and got dressed. I grabbed my coat and hat and stepped outside. My nose froze in the morning air. The sun was half an hour above the hill east of the bunkhouse. The sky was jaybird blue and cloudless. A perfect day.

When I got to John's kitchen a fire was waiting in the stove. John's Russian wolfhound, Benedick, was curled up beside it. He raised his head and wagged his tail when I came in. I fixed biscuits, huevos rancheros, rashers, frijoles refritos, and coffee. I tossed Benedick a rasher and a biscuit then rang the bell outside. John and the hands came in and sat at the table.

"Why're we going to Lincoln?" one of the hands asked. Lincoln was a two-day ride trailing stock.

"It's complicated," John said. "You remember when Emil Fritz died a couple of years ago? He was Lawrence Murphy's partner. He had a ten-thousand-dollar insurance policy naming his siblings as beneficiaries, but the insurance company wouldn't pay out the policy. Fritz's sister hired my partner Mac to collect the insurance money. Mac sued and got the money, then he paid his fees and expenses and gave what was left to the beneficiaries. Murphy now claims that Fritz owed him money. He says that Mac should have paid him with the insurance money before Mac paid himself. So he filed a claim against Mac, and he's trying to collect by attaching my property. He wants my cattle as payment for his claim. The judge agrees with him."

"I ain't no abogado," Dick Brewer said, "but I don't see how your cattle can settle Murphy's beef with the Fritz estate."

John laid aside his knife and fork and leaned back in his chair.

"Mac assures me they can't. If Murphy has a legitimate claim it's against the Fritz estate. The insurance money wasn't part of the estate. It belongs to the insurance beneficiaries, not Fritz's heirs. Mac collected his fees from the insurance money, not the Fritz estate. The claim against Mac is bogus.

"But even if Murphy did have a legitimate claim against Mac he has no right to my cattle. Mac and I are partners in the mercantile business, not the cattle business. Murphy convinced the judge that Mac has a half interest in my cattle. Mac told the judge that I'm the sole owner, but the judge didn't believe him. Instead he gave Murphy my cattle."

"Anyone wants your cattle better act quick," Dick said. "We don't get rain and grass this spring you won't have enough beef for a barbeque."

"Why we taking the horses and mules to Dick's?" Rob Widenmann asked.

"Sheriff Brady executed a writ for my cattle. He could show up any time. I don't want a fight, but I don't want to lose my horses and mules. Murphy has already overreached. The insurance was for only ten thousand dollars, but the writ's for all the cattle and they are worth twice that much. Brady will take any livestock he can find. If he takes the horses and mules I won't see them again. Dick can hide them at his ranch. Hopefully, when the wrangling is over Murphy's claim will be cleared up and I'll get my cattle back."

"Believe I'll have another huevo, Billy," Fred said, holding out his plate. "A dog biscuit too. Leave off them rashers. They taste like a dead skunk. How come you favor dog biscuits 'stead of Gauss's tortillas anyway?"

"Aunt Cat taught me how to bake them," I said, thumping a biscuit on his plate. "Surprised you ain't asking for fry bread. Chickasaws eat fry bread don't they?"

"We eat fry bread. Yeah, fry bread once in a while ain't a bad idea. It would give these dumbass cowhands a taste of Chickasaw. Maybe they wouldn't be so ignorant."

"I've eat fry bread," Rob said. "Had some at Miz Godfroy's a few days back. It ain't bad."

"There goes your argument, Fred. Rob's eaten fry bread and he's as ignorant as ever."

"I'm surprised Murphy's coming after you," Henry said. "I hear his guts are punky as a rotten log. He's already half a leg in the ground. Folks say he's drinking hisself to death so's he won't die of gut rot."

"You are not far from the truth," John said. "Murphy's cancer is killing him. Jimmy Dolan is running the business now, and he wants a war."

"So this campaign for your livestock ain't about insurance money?" Dick said.

"It's just an excuse. What is really at stake is the contract to sell beef to the army. I get my cattle from John Chisum at a good price. I can undercut Murphy. Murphy and Dolan want rid of the competition, permanently. That's why he's after the cattle."

"Dolan's the pissant to start a war," Dick said. "He's a flesh-eating maggot with the black heart of a banker. He'll shoot you for pesos."

"I know. He pulled a gun on me after the last court hearing. He baited me, calling me a coward."

"What'd you do?"

"Ignored him."

"Be careful, John. Dolan'll plug you in the back if he's of a mind."

"Jesse Evans got plugged in the butt a few days back," I said.

"I thought Jesse was in the calaboose for rustling," Dick said as he stood up from the table. "Did he bust out?"

"Brady let him out. Said he escaped, but he couldn't escape from that cellar without a pickax and shovel. No doubt the sheriff has plans for him. Hope it don't involve you none, John."

By then everyone had left the table. Most of the boys carried their plates and cups to the wash bucket on the sideboard, but Rob and Middleton headed straight for the door.

"Hey, you bungholes, don't leave your dishes on the table. I'm the cook, not your ma."

Middleton waved his middle finger, but him and Rob came back and picked up their dishes. Middleton set his plate on the floor beside Benedick. The wolfhound wiped it clean.

"Thanks, Middleton. I'll save that plate for you."

CHAPTER 2 **Tunstall**

My Dear Parents, I am still alive & well . . . You have no idea of the press of business & annoyance I am staggering under.

—JOHN H. TUNSTALL, LETTER, NOVEMBER 16, 1877

SHORTLY AFTER BREAKFAST WE WERE saddled up, waiting on Rob Widenmann to take off for Lincoln. I'd packed leftover biscuits, jerky, coffee, and oranges John'd gotten from California. First oranges I'd ever seen. I put the provisions in the buckboard. We were taking the buckboard to bring back supplies and books for the ranch. John bought books from a drummer in Colorado. He ordered books from London too and had them delivered to his mercantile.

In a few minutes Rob brought around the string of horses and mules to leave at Dick Brewer's ranch. All but one mule belonged to John. Ownership of the odd mule was up for negotiation. Jesse Evans said it was hisn. I said it was mine. Jesse knew the mule was at John's. I figured he'd be in the posse when they came for the lot. Me and Jesse'd been friends and had rustled a few head together, but we'd disagreed about the mule. I didn't intend to give it up without a fight.

"Sheriff Brady may be on his way," John said. "He'll come down the Lincoln Road. I hope we don't run into him before we get to Lincoln. We'll take the Ham Mills Road if we reach the cutoff before he does."

"Okay, boss," Dick said. "We'd best be going."

We started down the ranch road, Dick and Rob in the lead. John followed in the buckboard with Benedick loping beside him. I brought up the rear, trailing stock. My horse Buck was a gift from John. He was an unusual buckskin color and a fine compadre.

The ranch road ran beside the Río Feliz most of the way. Cottonwoods lined the river on both sides. The few piñons and junipers scattered across the hillsides weren't much taller than a man on horseback, but some of the cottonwoods were huge. Five men, maybe six, couldn't wrap their arms around the trunks.

"Hey, Biscuit Boy," Dick called. "One of them álamos would warm the bunkhouse for the winter."

"You cut it, I'll burn it," I said, "but it'll pop like a Gatling gun and stink like Rob pissed on it. While you're snoring, sparks'll set you ablaze."

When we got to the Lincoln Road we turned north. It'd snowed a couple of days earlier. The road was rutted from wagon wheels and had froze solid during the night. The horses picked a path around the ruts, but John was in for a butt-busting ride in the buckboard. When the road split we took the Ham Mills fork into the mountains. It was shorter and steeper, but the rougher terrain added hours to the trip. We left the piñons and junipers and got into the ponderosas. Late in the afternoon we were riding through scrub oaks when a flock of turkeys crossed the road. Must of been a dozen. Benedick took off, silent as a spook.

"Supper," Dick said.

He pulled his Winchester from its scabbard and headed into the woods. Rob followed. I reached for my Winchester and spurred Buck around the wagon. The flock ran a few more yards then took to the air, Benedick close behind. The birds broke out of the oaks and glided down the mountain. We spread out. I'd gone a couple of hundred paces looking for the birds to light when I heard a rifle crack behind me. Figured John'd seen another flock, but then I remembered that he'd left his rifle at the ranch. In a moment there was more gunfire.

I turned Buck and started back toward the ruckus. Hadn't gone far before I saw John standing in the buckboard. Tom Hill from Jesse Evans' gang and Buck Morton, foreman of Dolan's cow camp, rode up to him with a posse close behind. I recognized a few, Jesse among them.

John was turning around when Morton fired point blank. John fell sideways out of the buckboard. Hill shot him again when he hit the ground. I reined up and dropped off of Buck. Dick and Rob were coming up behind me. I waved them down and put my finger to my lips. Benedick raced past before I could grab him.

"They got John," I whispered. "Looks like maybe a dozen."

"Damn," Dick muttered. "There goes Benedick. Shit."

"What now?" Rob said.

Dick motioned and we backed down the hill.

Morton had climbed off his horse about the time Benedick broke out of the woods.

"Look out, Buck," Hill yelled.

Morton spun around as Benedick leapt and Hill fired. Benedick crashed into Morton. Both fell to the ground.

"¡Puta madre! Where'd that cabrón come from!"

Morton scrabbled out from under the wolfhound.

"Thanks, Hill. He's one fierce sonofabitch."

The string had broken and scattered at the sound of gunfire. Two of the mules cut into the woods. Morton took John's bay out of the traces.

"Hill, you and Evans round up the rest of the stock. Let's get outta here."

Hill went after the horses down the road. Jesse followed the mules into the woods. I raised my Winchester in case Jesse crossed our tracks in the snow.

"Got my mule without a fight," Jesse said when he emerged with the mules. "Too bad about you, Billy Boy."

When all the stock was back together, Morton grabbed Benedick by the hind legs and swung him hard, whacking his head against a tree.

"That'll fix you, you weird shit. We're done here, boys. Let's go."

Morton swung onto the saddle, and the posse took off at a trot toward Lincoln, our stock in tow. We waited till they were out of earshot, then came out of the woods. John was balled up in a hump on the ground. A hole in his temple was leaking. Blood stained the back of his jacket.

"No need to kill him." Rob said. "He didn't have no gun."

Dick and Rob lifted John and laid him in the back of the buckboard.

I picked up Benedick and half dragged him out of the woods. Rob helped me lay him beside John.

"What now?" Rob said. "Back to the ranch, bury 'em?"

"We started for Lincoln," Dick said. "That ain't changed. Now we've got a murder to report."

"Two," I said. "And two sidewinders to send to hell."

Dick didn't say anything. He pulled at an Apache charm hanging from his neck. I backed Buck into the traces and climbed onto the buckboard. There was blood on the seat. I reached for a canteen and saw John looking past me into the woods. I closed his eyes then flooded the seat with water and wiped it off with my sleeve. I looked at Dick and Rob then giddyuped Buck toward Lincoln.

A short while later we crossed a gap in the mountains and left the snow behind. Toward evening we found a flat spot in the ponderosas to bed down for the night. The trunks were broad as a man's outstretched arms and rose thirty or more feet before putting out branches. There were grasses and weeds and small shrubs but mostly the ground was covered with pine straw.

I unloaded the supplies and gathered pine straw and branches to build a fire. Rob fed the horses. Dick scouted up the road to make sure the posse was out of earshot. He returned with an armload of firewood. I scraped away pine straw and dug a fire pit. I always carried pine sticks soaked in coal oil for starting a fire. When I got the fire going I made coffee and set out biscuits, jerky, oranges. We sat on logs and ate in silence.

After we finished Rob said, "Wished we'd shot one of them turkeys."

"If we had," Dick said, "we'd be in the wagon back yonder waiting on the buzzards."

That pretty much ended the conversation. I stretched out a tarp where the pine straw was deep, and we laid out our bedrolls. We hadn't seen a cloud all day. The temperature tumbled when the sun went down. Then the moon came up. Somewhere off in the night a lobo howled. Another answered. We huddled round the fire. Had enough firewood to last the night.

"Whadda we do about the bodies?" Rob said. "Won't they draw wolves or bears or shit?"

"It ain't bodies," Dick said, "It's John and Benedick. They won't draw varmints. It's bitter cold tonight. They won't stink no worse'n you."

We sat up awhile talking about John and the ranch and the troubles ahead. Dick finally called it a night, but me and Rob were too fired up to sleep. I threw more logs on the fire, then me and Rob listened to Dick snore for the next few hours.

"You ever think about dying?" Rob asked.

"Some maybe. Not much."

"You afraid to die?"

"No. Don't want to. But I have to some day. Expect it'll be sooner than later."

The moon had climbed high overhead. Another lobo called from a far-off ridge.

"I'm afraid to die. Why ain't you?"

"I figure to go out with a bullet. Like John. Won't see it coming. One minute I'll be standing there, next minute I'll be gone. No fuss, no pain. Or very little. Of course, if I'm gutshot, lying in an arroyo baking in the sun for a day or two, that could get ugly. Get one of them logs. This fire's about to fade."

Rob handed me a couple of logs and I laid them on the fire. The heat burned my legs. I backed away and sat down again.

"Suppose you die at the hands of a Comanch taking his time?"

"That's a different proposition. I ain't afraid to die but I am skittish about the how. If I was buried to my chin in a fire pit, my eyeballs peeled, or staked out naked like a blanket on an anthill, my privates sewed in my mouth, I'd sure as hell wish I'd shot myself."

"It terrifies me."

"I don't speculate it much. My grandpap said that most of the bad things he worried about never happened. If they did they weren't that bad."

"He'd of been wrong about John."

CHAPTER 3 The Wake

The public regard this as the most inexcusable murder that has ever taken place here, but unless you cause the matter to be looked into I have but small hopes of the matter being properly prosecuted. . . . I have written to Tunstall's father.

—ALEXANDER A. MCSWEEN, LETTER TO BRITISH ENVOY, FEBRUARY 25, 1878

WHEN I WOKE AT FIRST light a raven prowling around our gear was staring at me. I tossed a pinecone at him and he flew off. I made us a quick breakfast, then we packed up and were on our way.

Shortly after noon we rode into Lincoln. It's little more than a flat spot beside the Río Bonito, fenced in by cornfields and barren hills. Back then it had a hotel, a courthouse, a calaboose, a few mercantiles, and a dozen or so houses. A couple of hundred families lived within a day's ride, most of them Mex. It had a stone tower, a torreón, for defense against Apaches. Today I reckon the town's pretty much the same. A few more houses. McSween's house is gone. The San Juan Mission Church was built after I left. Your brother told me about it.

When we pulled up at McSween's, Mac came out. We told him what happened.

"My God," Mac said. "Lawrence Murphy and Jimmy Dolan did this?"

"His boys shot John like a polecat," Dick said. "They'll be after you next."

"After me? Great God almighty. I should never have left Wichita."

Mac was silent for a moment, then he said, "There's nothing I can do about it now. We've got John to take care of. Sue's not here. We had guests this morning. Dr. Taylor Ealy and his wife. They just moved here. Sue took them to Fort Stanton. Bring John into the parlor. Do something about Benedick too."

Mac and Rob and Dick lifted John from the buckboard and carried him into the parlor while I dragged Benedick to the backyard.

Mac's house backed up to the Río Bonito. The house was U-shaped. The McSweens lived in the left wing, the Shields in the right. A parlor joined the two wings and faced the street.

Elizabeth Shield was Sue's sister. Her husband was a lawyer like Mac. Mac'd offered him a share in the business. Mac didn't need a partner but Sue needed her sister. Sue's Spanish was poor and she wanted a woman to talk to. Promise of a partnership was enough to get the Shields to abandon Missouri for New Mexico.

The house was adobe but Sue had fixed it up like her house in Wichita. Paintings on the walls, curtains on the windows, a piano in the parlor. The parlor was my favorite room. Lined with books. I spent many an hour there. Mac had three or four times as many books as John. I was interested in most everything and read most any book I came across. Mac had law books, lots of them. I ignored them. But he had books on animals, history, novels, poetry. If I was in Lincoln and wasn't running errands or running after señoritas, I was shooting targets or reading in Mac's parlor. *The Iliad* was my favorite. Read it twice. About the Greeks and the Trojan War in the old days. Achilles was the hero. Back then I figured he was a warrior to model your life after. Today he seems more like a Comanche.

Tunstall's mercantile was in the building next door. John kept sleeping quarters there. The building housed Mac's law office and a bank run by Mac and John Chisum.

"A couple of you fellas go to the stable and grab some boards along the back wall," Mac said.

Rob and me went through the kitchen and out the back to the stable a few steps off of Sue's kitchen. Under a tarp behind Mac's wagon we found a stack of pine boards. They were long and wide and heavy. We chose two and brought them back to the parlor one at a time. When we came in with the second board, Mac had moved the piano and chairs back to the bookshelves. He brought in two benches from the kitchen and set them a few feet apart in the center of the room. We laid the boards on the benches to make a low table. Then the four of us lifted John off the floor and laid him on the boards.

"What about John's killers?" Dick said.

"They'll have to wait. First off we've got to bury John," Mac said. "Benedick too. Rob, can you ride to Fort Stanton and ask Lieutenant Appel to do a postmortem? He's a surgeon. Ask Dr. Ealy to come too. He's a preacher. He can do the funeral."

Rob nodded.

"We need to get word to John Chisum," Mac said.

"I'll look around town for someone to hunt him up," Rob said. "If I can't find nobody I'll head to his ranch when I get back."

"I'll send a letter to the Tunstalls," Mac said. "John was their only son. It's tragic. John was playing by the rules of London gentlemen. He was too naïve for this country."

"Murphy and Dolan own the sheriff," Dick said. "They're all in cahoots. There's no law here. Shooting John wasn't just murder. It was an act of war. Murphy and Dolan want the territory for their own selves. Before John come along I was up to my ass in hock to L. G. Murphy and Company. Murdering John skewered me. Skewered all us ranchers. I expect we can round up an army quick. String up them sonsabitches. Brady won't do nothing. He ain't no sheriff. He's a poor shakes of a potato farmer who couldn't make a living in the old country."

"There's still a little law left," Mac said. "Neither the justice of the peace nor the constable is a member of the Murphy faction. I'll talk to them tomorrow. Get warrants and swear in a couple of you fellows as deputy constables. Billy, you saw Hill and Morton shoot John. You can tell it to a grand jury. You can testify about the rest of the posse too. They're accessories."

We continued to talk throughout the day while John laid on the cooling board. Late in the afternoon Dick and me left the house to dig a grave for Benedick behind Tunstall's. I said a few words and promised Benedick that Morton and Hill would be following him soon.

Word spread about the killing. Boys began showing up at Mac's door. The first to arrive was Henry Antrim. He was my oldest friend. Everybody called him Kid. He was about my height but thin as shoe leather. His arms looked like twigs in winter. We'd spent a few years together in Silver City. Kid was from New York. He never knew his pa. His mother Catherine took him and his brother west when he was about ten. They settled in Denver with a guy named Antrim. Catherine and Antrim married, moved to Silver City. That's where I met him. When I left home for Arizona Territory, Kid went to Lincoln and worked on a ranch not far from John's. He's the one got me the job with John.

Kid'd stopped by Murphy's mercantile on his way into town. He was surprised because the sign over the store said "Dolan and Company" instead of "Murphy and Company." A dozen men were holed up inside. Three or four of them reached for their six-shooters when Kid walked through the door. He didn't know what was up. Said they looked like coyotes on a kill. He didn't ask about the new sign. Just backed out and came on to Tunstall's. Found us at Mac's.

By nightfall near forty boys had crowded into Mac's parlor. Fred Waite was there too. He'd come on from John's ranch that morning. Said he had a bad feeling after the posse left. It was all Mac could do to keep the boys from heading home to gather up Sharps and Springfields and Winchesters.

Dick talked war to anyone who'd listen. I figure he's the reason it's called the Lincoln County War to this day. A few years earlier the Horrell brothers rampaged through Lincoln County killing near as many people. No one called their time of terror a war. No one much remembers the Horrells. Most everyone they killed was Mexican. That's the difference I reckon.

I didn't see the Lincoln County War the way Dick did. Figured it was more like the Horrell troubles. Varmints'd killed the best man I knew. I wanted to string them up. Dick was smarter than the rest of us. He saw more at stake. He saw death like a duster blowing through the county. He was right. About every ranch within a two-day ride of Lincoln would lose family or friends over the next couple of years. Dick didn't dream that his ranch would be the first to feel the loss.

CHAPTER 4 **Morton**

I am not afraid at all of their killing me, but if they should do so, I wish that the matter should be investigated and the parties dealt with according to law. If you do not hear from me in four days after receipt of this, I would like you to make inquiries about the affair.

—WILLIAM S. MORTON, LETTER TO H. H. MARSHALL, MARCH 8, 1878

SUE MCSWEEN RETURNED HOME SOON as she learned of John's death. During the night the last of the boys left McSween's for their farms and ranches. Me and John's hands bedded down in the backyard. Preacher Ealy and the post surgeon stayed the night at the fort and rode in next morning.

While the surgeon performed the postmortem, Mac sent me and Fred Waite to the justice of the peace for warrants. The constable deputized us, then him and me and Fred went to Dolan's store looking for Morton and Hill.

A dozen men looked up when we entered, but my eyes were fixed on the open end of Sheriff Brady's double-barrel shotgun.

"Ya lads be lookin' for trouble?" he said.

"We've got warrants for William Scott Morton and Thomas Henry Hill," the constable said. "For the murder of John Henry Tunstall."

"Have ya now. Well I be holdin' warrants for the three of ya."

"What for?"

"Waite and Bonney for thievin' and you for blatherin'."

"Show me your warrants."

"These barrels be all the warrants I be needin'. Grab their guns, lads."

Morton stepped up to take our hardware. He was three or four years older than me, a foot taller, and half my size heavier. We'd worked together rounding up cattle on the Pecos. I used to consider him a compadre.

"I'll send you to hell, Morton," I said as he reached for my Winchester.

We glared at each other, both gripping the Winchester.

"You're next, Bonney," he said. "Right after McSween."

I turned loose of the rifle and handed him my six-shooter.

With the shotgun at our backs Sherriff Brady walked us to the calaboose. The cell was a dug-out pit, five paces on a side, below the sheriff's office. A trapdoor opened to a rope ladder into the cell. The walls were made of logs. The floor was dirt. The ceiling gave us half a foot of clearance. The only light came through cracks in the overhead floorboards. Dirt rained down whenever anyone walked around in the sheriff's office. Half a dozen bunks lined three walls. The fourth wall was the latrine. A couple of slop buckets sat beside it, but aims were often bad. Jesse Evans was the last guest. He'd been gone a week. The cell stank of piss and shit.

"You've no law to hold us," the constable said. "McSween'll get us out soon enough."

"More likely he'll be beddin' here with ya soon enough," Brady said.

A few hours later Brady let the constable out but me and Fred stayed near a week. I've been locked up before but never in such a privy. Like being in the belly of a cave. I slept without thought of day or night. At times I wasn't sure if I was awake or asleep, especially when I saw things. Avoided the latrine but I had to use it some. Couldn't always tell where it was. Especially the slop buckets. Once I pissed on a bunk until Fred yelled at me.

Brady brought us gruel once a day. We ate with our hands. Couldn't see what we were eating.

"Believe you'll favor my rashers after eating this pig shit," I said a couple of days into our stay.

"Won't never grouse about your grub again," Fred said.

After John's funeral a dozen of the boys came to the calaboose demanding our release. Brady tried staring them down. When that didn't work he turned us loose. Handed us our Winchesters and gave me a single-action Colt .44 with wooden grips.

"This ain't mine," I said. "This is a kid's toy. The barrel is shorter than my little finger. Mine's an ivory-handle Thunderer."

"Thunderer me arse."

"I ain't taking this piece of crap."

"I can give ya more crap if ya like."

"Leave it, Billy," Fred said.

"I ain't afraid of you," I said to Brady. "You keep my Colt, you'll regret it. If you're still breathing when I collect it."

"Threatenin' me are ya?"

"Not threatening. Promising."

"I still be holdin' warrants for cattle thievin'. I can kick your arse in the kip till Judge Bristol arrives."

"Let's go, Billy," Fred said.

Fred was right. I couldn't take another day in that calaboose. As we walked to Mac's house I swore I'd get my Colt back.

John Tunstall's cowhands—Dick Brewer, John Middleton, Rob Widenmann, and Henry Brown—were waiting for us at Mac's. Frank MacNab and José Chavez were there too. MacNab was a cattle detective working for one of the stock associations. He had a reputation as a killer but the law never pinned a killing on him.

José was the best man with a six-shooter that I ever saw. After Bob Ford bragged about killing Jesse James, José challenged him to a gunfight. What I heard, and it wasn't from José, is that Ford turned tail like a coyote and snuck into the sagebrush.

Shortly after me and Fred got to Mac's, Doc Scurlock and Charlie Bowdre showed up. Doc had been a dentist. He quit practicing after he lost his front teeth to a bullet in a card game. The other fella wasn't so lucky. Doc and Charlie were partners in a ranch on the Ruidoso.

Frank and George Coe were the last to arrive. They were cousins. Had farmed and ranched together in New Mexico and Colorado. Both were handy with rifles. Especially George.

Sue made coffee for us while we debated what to do about John's killers.

"Brady's protecting the bastards," Dick Brewer said. "Ain't no law here. We're John's only justice. Let's get the varmints ourselves."

Everyone agreed. We took an oath of loyalty. Swore to bring in Hill and Morton and the rest of the posse. Someone suggested calling us Regulators. We chose Dick as leader. At one time or another there were near fifty Regulators, but the boys who took the oath that day made up the core.

Mac didn't say much. He didn't take the oath either. He was near terrified. He asked if he was in danger.

"Hell yes," Dick said. "Said so when we brought John in. Danger's doubled now."

I told Mac what Morton said the day I was arrested.

"You're next, Mac. His meaning couldn't of been clearer."

"What should I do?" Mac said. "I can't leave. I've got too much at stake here."

"Hole up till this stew settles," Dick said.

"My hermano has a casita in the Pajaritos," José Chavez said. "It is not much, but Jesus will let you stay. You helped him when Murphy tried to take his ranch. He could not pay you then. He can pay you now."

Mac and Sue talked it over. Sue'd stay behind to look after the house while his brother-in-law'd look after the business. Mac wrote out a will. After dark, him and José slipped away. The rest of us bedded down in the backyard.

Next morning while Sue fixed breakfast we sat at the kitchen table planning our first foray. Bill McCloskey showed up wanting to join us.

"He's one of Morton's amigos," I said. "He's on the wrong side."

"You were one of Morton's amigos," Dick said. "I reckon Bill can come. We can use an extra gun."

Dick went to the justice of the peace and the constable's offices to pick up warrants and get hisself made deputy constable. When he came back he swore in the rest of us. Dick wanted to go after Morton first. Morton was foreman of Jimmy Dolan's cow camp on the Black River. He'd be easiest to find. We mounted up and headed for Seven Rivers.

That evening we camped in a cottonwood grove beside the Río Peñasco. I built a fire and we sat around eating supper, telling tales, and speculating the future. It was clear from the conversation that most of the boys were greenhorns even though some were close to thirty. A few were carrying six-shooters. The rest had Winchesters or Springfields. They left their rifles with their saddles when they turned out their horses. I picked up a couple of logs, put them on the fire, and dropped in a few cartridges. Charlie Bowdre saw what I done. When the cartridges exploded, all the boys but Charlie cut for the trees, abandoning their rifles. When they realized the joke they filtered back to the fire.

"I was impressed with your nerves, boys," Charlie said to the embarrassed cowhands, "but where was your hardware?"

Early next morning we continued along the Río Peñasco. As the sun was coming up we spotted five hombres around a campfire near the junction of the Peñasco and the Río Pecos. One of them fired his rifle at us.

"Morton," I said. "The one clambering into the saddle's Frank Baker. He was in Morton's posse when they came after John."

A Seven Rivers boy was also with them. I didn't know the other two birds. Baker was a member of Jesse Evans' gang. I'd rode with him when we were chasing cattle around the Chisum ranch. A few years older'n me. Mean sonofabitch.

The hombres mounted and raced toward the Pecos. We opened fire and gave chase. Bullets flew in both directions. I emptied my six-shooter twice. When we reached the Pecos the two strangers splashed across the river and headed north toward Roswell. The other three turned south toward Seven Rivers. We let the strangers go and continued after Morton. The Seven Rivers boy's horse stumbled, throwing the cowboy into the tule. He wasn't part of Morton's posse. We raced past. Wished I'd put a bullet in him. A couple of months later he killed a Regulator.

A few miles on, Morton's horse gave out. Him and Baker reined up among the cottonwoods. We cut into the cottonwoods and dismounted, stepping up the gunfire, but no one was hit. After a few minutes Baker and Morton's shots slowed to a trickle then petered out.

"Hold your fire," Dick called.

"Is that you, Dick?" Morton said.

"Yeah, it's me."

"You got us outnumbered. If we come out with our hands up will you hold your fire?"

"No one's gonna shoot."

"You ain't talking for me," I said. "Soon as Morton's in the clear I'll ream out both his eyes."

"Cool down, Billy. We got to do this legal. Come on out, Morton. There'll be no more shooting. You'll hang soon enough."

"Bonney don't sound of the same mind."

I shook my head.

"Billy's okay. He won't shoot."

"We're coming out."

Morton stepped into a clearing, holding his six-shooter and Winchester by the barrels. Baker did the same. Dick took their hardware. We mounted up and turned north toward the Chisum ranch.

We spent the night at the ranch. Baker and Morton were tied up in the bunkhouse. Four of us took turns guarding them. I volunteered for the last watch, hoping Morton might try for a break by then, but nothing happened. Him and Baker were too trussed up.

Next morning we headed toward Lincoln. Before we got to Roswell, John Middleton rode up. He was one of John Tunstall's hands.

"Word's out about you going after Morton," Middleton said. "Sheriff's rounding up a posse to head you off."

"Thanks," Dick said. "The posse'll be coming down the Roswell Road. We'll take the Military Road through the Capitans."

"I'd as soon shoot it out," I said. "We can clean up a passel of killers in a slick. Nice and legal."

"They'll have a good idea how many we are," Dick said. "They'll send an army if they have to. We made a good haul yesterday. Let's not risk it."

"How the hell did they get wind of us," Frank MacNab said.

Believe I told you he was a stock detective. Had a ranch near Tunstall's.

"No one knew we was going except us. Someone's talked."

That evening when we got to Agua Negra Canyon, MacNab rode up beside McCloskey.

"I've been wondering how folks figured we'd be hunting Morton at his cow camp," he said. "Then I recalled you saying you were going to the jakes and we should wait on you. You spent a long time in them jakes. Must of been Dolan's."

McCloskey glared at MacNab then went for his gun. MacNab was a step ahead of him. He fired over his pommel. McCloskey fell out of the saddle. During the fracas Morton and Baker bolted for the trees. I drew my six-shooter and fired twice. It was near dark and my horse was skittish. Wasn't sure what I hit. Baker fell first. Morton made it to the trees but was leaning out of his saddle. His head smashed into a ponderosa as his horse ran past.

Horses started crowhopping. Middleton flipped out of the saddle and landed on his back, fending off hooves.

"Hold your fire! Hold your fire! Who's shooting?" Dick yelled.

"I called out McCloskey for ratting," MacNab said. "He went for his six-shooter. I shot him. Morton and Baker made a break for it. Billy got 'em before they hit the woods."

"Damn!" Dick said. "Are they dead?"

"McCloskey's gutshot. He'll be dead by morning. Don't know about Morton or Baker. Neither of 'em look good."

MacNab got off his horse and walked over to Baker.

"Hit in the withers. Nice shot, Billy."

Then he checked on Morton.

"Him too. In the back. Head looks like a busted pumpkin. His ole lady won't be kissing him goodbye."

"Shit," Dick said.

"Couldn't be helped," I said. "We knew a polecat was amongst us. If MacNab hadn't flushed him out, could be you and me on the ground instead of Morton and Baker."

"McCloskey weren't in Morton's posse," Dick said. "We ain't got cause for killing him."

"McCloskey went for his six-shooter. That's cause enough. We've plenty of witnesses."

"Folks'll be screaming for blood. Brady'll come after MacNab. He could hang."

"Say Morton grabbed McCloskey's gun, shot him, made a break for it."

"They won't buy it. McCloskey and Morton were amigos."

"Don't matter what they buy. Long as we agree, they can't prove otherwise. Any other explanation is pissing in the wind."

We argued into the night. By morning we'd settled it. Baker, not Morton, grabbed McCloskey's gun, shot him, and made a break for it. I shot Morton and Baker as they were getting away.

Not that it mattered. While we were hunting Morton, the governor revoked Dick's commission and fired the justice of the peace. Our warrants were dead letters. We were all outlaws then.

CHAPTER 5 **Brewer**

Peace to your ashes, Dick! as you were familiarly called. Sweet and pleasant be your slumbers! Ever green and fresh be your memory. Some may malign you, but that will not disturb you, for when the mist has cleared away and the horizon of truth is clearly seen, even they will be shamed to silence.

—RICHARD BREWER OBITUARY, *Cimarron News and Press*, APRIL 18, 1878

THE GOOD NEWS WAS THAT Tom Hill was dead. I hoped John Tunstall and Benedick were up there watching. Hill died the same day Buck Morton did. A half-breed sheep drover caught Hill and Jesse Evans raiding the drover's camp near Tularosa. Hill and Evans were fixated on thievery and didn't see the drover return to camp. He shot both of them. Hill's wound was fatal. Evans was hit in the lights but he got away. After he shot the drover.

Evans was a tough sonofabitch. He could catch more lead and stay in the saddle better'n any boy I knew. He rode near sixty miles to Fort Stanton. After the post surgeon patched him up the army put him in the stockade till Sheriff Brady came for him.

There was more good news. After the governor's proclamation making Brady and Judge Bristol the only law in the county, Dolan got drunk to celebrate. Not that he needed a reason. While he was celebrating he dismounted from a moving horse. His foot hung in the stirrup. The horse near ripped it off. I was sorry he felt no pain but took satisfaction watching him hobble around Lincoln like a three-legged dog.

A few weeks later I was back in Lincoln for a hearing. Mac had been charged with embezzling the Fritz estate. I'd been called as a witness to John Tunstall's murder, but I wasn't about to show myself. I waited in Tunstall's store to hear how everything played out. The town had swelled by half as witnesses and defendants and jurymen filled the beds at the Wortley Hotel and any other lodging they could find. It was a cold and rainy morning. Lincoln was a hog wallow. When Brady showed up he said the court got the date wrong. Court wouldn't open for another week. Folks were horn-mad.

When the boys left the courthouse they came over to Tunstall's to report on the happenings. The store and Mac's house were next to each other. Since John's murder, Mac had built a four-foot adobe wall bordering Main Street in front of both buildings.

Henry Brown was looking out the store window when he saw Brady coming down the street. Word was out that Brady aimed to arrest me and Fred Waite for appropriating cattle.

"Here comes your compadre, Billy," Henry said. "Hindman and Mathews are with him."

George Hindman and Billy Mathews were deputy sheriffs. They were in Morton's posse when he murdered John. Hindman had a farm on the Hondo. He was a cripple. Old Ephraim about got him years earlier up in the Sacramentos. Mathews was a braggart and a bully. Him and me'd had a fracas a week earlier. I'd called him out for John's murder and was reaching for my six-shooter when Fred Waite stopped my hand. We walked away. But I swore I'd get the sonofabitch.

"Brady's got warrants for us," I said. "Probably in his pocket. I'm replevying mine."

Henry and Fred and me and Kid Antrim ducked out the backdoor and came up behind the adobe wall blocking our view from the street. We could hear mud sucking at the men's boots. When Fred thought they were close enough he gave a nod. We raised up and fired. I aimed at Mathews. He was already running and I missed. I fired again but the .44

misfired. Most of the boys were aiming for Brady. The sheriff sat down in the mud then keeled over backward, his head landing in horse shit. Hindman was on his knees.

Fred and me jumped over the wall and ran toward Brady. In the mud beside him was my ivory-handled double-action .41. I'd given twenty-five dollars for that Colt in San Antone and was happy to get it back. I was faster and truer with it than with the short-barrel shit-shooter Brady gave me when I got out of the calaboose.

While admiring my prize I felt a burn in the butt. I turned and saw Mathews duck behind the corner of Sisneros's casa. Fred let out a yelp. The slug took a chunk out of me and clipped Fred in the leg. We hobbled back to the store.

When the shooting started, folks on the street scattered. Preacher Ealy'd run into the street and was looking after Hindman who was still kneeling. Me and Fred cut through Tunstall's store and out the back to the corral. We figured Mathews would round up a posse and be after us quick. The rain would delay him some. We saddled up and skinned out for San Patricio.

We spent the next two days at Jesus Chavez's place in the Pajaritos, licking our wounds like a pair of dogs. Next morning Dick Brewer showed up with the boys. He said that Mathews couldn't get up a posse. He also said that some of the posse who'd murdered John were hiding out on the Mescalero Reservation. It was a good time to go after them. Fred and me saddled up and rode down the Tularosa Road to the reservation with the Regulators. A few hours later we stopped at Miz Godfroy's for dinner at Blazer's Mill.

Blazer's Mill is a settlement on the Río Tularosa. It was called South Fork before Doc Blazer bought a sawmill and house there shortly after the War between the States. Never was much there. A post office. Half a dozen houses. Up the road from the sawmill Doc had put up a two-story building for defense against Apaches. The adobe walls were two-feet thick. The doors were thick as my fist. Portholes under the eaves looked out on all sides.

Fred Godfroy, the Indian agent, leased part of the building for an office and quarters. Godfroy's missus rented rooms and ran a chow hall there. Dinner was four bits. Her apple pie was the best in the territory. If you wanted a slice you had to arrive early. Regulars had pie for breakfast.

Miz Godfroy didn't allow guns. Never saw the rule broke. I've seen bitter enemies scowling across the table, but nary a one would go for his hardware or lay low in an arroyo afterward to ambush an enemy. Miz Godfroy commanded that kind of respect.

We put our horses in the corral then crossed the creek on a log bridge and went up to the chow hall. John Middleton got the short straw and stayed with the hardware while the rest of us went in.

We'd hardly sat down when Middleton rushed in.

"Buckshot Roberts is in the post office."

Charlie Bowdre knocked over his chair getting up.

"That sumbitching rooster's mine, by god," he said. "Today I'm bedding him with the devil. Few days ago me and him traded lead in San Pat. He shot my horse!"

Buckshot Roberts was a penny-ante outlaw. He was in Morton's posse when they murdered John. Dick had a warrant for him. He'd been a Texas Ranger. When the Rangers saw him for the thieving coyote that he was, they ran him out of the state. He became a bounty hunter. Rumor had it that Dolan was offering a hundred dollars for each of us. Dead preferably. Figured Roberts was out hunting us then.

"Easy, Charlie," Dick said. "The governor voided our warrants but maybe they're still good with the marshals. We'll take Roberts alive. Turn him over to the federals."

"I know Buckshot pretty good," Frank Coe said. "He's a neighbor. I'll talk to him. Believe I can bring him in."

The Coes were a tough breed but Frank was the toughest. He went after the Stockton gang after Port Stockton killed one of his friends. Frank killed Port then frequented Ike Stockton's bar, looking for the rest of the gang. One night one of the cousins came up behind him with a knife. Frank took the knife away from the ole boy and gutted him with it. Witnesses said it was a fair fight.

Dick Brewer told Frank to have at it with Roberts.

"He ain't going nowhere," Dick said.

Frank went down the hill to the post office as Roberts was coming out. The rest of us slipped out the front door, grabbed our guns, and ran down the hill to the back of the post office in case Roberts tried to skedaddle. Frank and Roberts were arguing.

"I ain't giving my guns to them skunk bears. I know what they done to Morton and Baker."

"They'll kill you sure if you make a break for it. Stick with me. I won't let 'em shoot you."

"You can't stop Bonney. They was a dozen holes in Buck Morton's back. Everybody knows what happened. Morton weren't trying to get away. It was murder, plain and simple. Bowdre and Bonney bushwhacked me in San Pat last week. I was lucky to get out alive."

"Sockdologizing sumbitch!" Charlie whispered. "That lying lowlife bushwhacked us. We wouldn't of knowed he was there if lead hadn't of whizzed past my ear."

Charlie stepped around the corner of the post office, his six-shooter drawn.

"Drop your Winchester, you shit-eating chingón. We're bringing you in."

Middleton and George Coe were fanning Charlie's back. Fred and me were in the rear, still limping from Mathews' bullet. Roberts swung his Winchester up to his waist. Charlie fired first, catching Roberts in the gut. Roberts pumped off three shots in a lick. One ricocheted off Charlie's belt buckle, snapping off George's trigger finger. Middleton caught one in the chest. I was grazed on the arm. We ducked for cover while Roberts stumbled across the road to Doc Blazer's house. Dick ran down the hill to the sawmill for a clear view of Doc's house. He dropped to the ground behind a pile of logs, raised his Winchester, and opened fire. He ducked below the logs to reload. When he raised up again, Roberts popped him in the eye, blowing out the back of his skull.

We were in a pickle. Dick was dead. John Middleton and George Coe were out of commission. Even gutshot, Roberts was deadly. At well over a hundred paces he'd taken out Dick when his eyebrows was barely visible above the log pile. We got Middleton and Coe into a wagon. One of

Doc's hands drove them to the doctor in Ruidoso. The rest of us figured we'd wait Roberts out.

That evening Lieutenant Appel, the Fort Stanton surgeon, showed up. Godfroy had wired the fort. He knew the doctor would come. Appel was engaged to his daughter.

"We've heard nothing from Roberts," I said. "Ain't too eager to look in on him."

"Believe he'll let me in," the lieutenant said.

Appel went down the road out of sight from Doc Blazer's house. He crossed over and came back up by the end of the house where there were no windows or doors. When he eased around to the front he called to Roberts.

"Mr. Roberts, I'm Lieutenant Daniel Appel of the United States Army. I'm the surgeon at Fort Stanton. Can you hear me?"

"Hear you fine, Lieutenant."

"How are you feeling?"

"Been better."

"Can I come in . . . without getting shot?"

"You alone?"

"Yessir."

"Suit yourself. I ain't much in a shooting mood anyways."

The lieutenant found Roberts lying on a mattress below the window. The mattress was soaked in blood.

"Let me look at your wounds, sir."

"Look as you like, Lieutenant. Ain't much to see. I've lost about all I had."

"I can wrap you up. Make you a mite more comfortable."

"Ain't sure comfortable's the right word. 'Preciate it though."

Appel came out of the house carrying Doc Blazer's Springfield, the one Roberts had used on Dick. He confirmed that Roberts was gutshot. Said Roberts had a few hours at most.

Dick had laid in the sun all day. No one was willing to get him while Roberts was dangerous. When Appel assured us Roberts' Winchester was out of ammunition, me and a couple of the boys went down to the log pile to retrieve Dick's body. Dick was still wearing an Apache charm around his neck. A rawhide ring hanging from four rawhide strings. A string of mescal beans hung from the ring. A Mescalero woman gave it to him. He'd found her near Tularosa with a broke leg. He brought her to Fort Stanton. Lieutenant Appel fixed her up. She told Dick the charm would bring him good luck. She was wrong about that.

I lifted the charm off of Dick and hung it around my neck. Not for luck. For resolve. I'd made a promise to John Tunstall. I owed Dick one too.

We carried Dick to the big house and laid him out in the Indian Agency office. The rest of us took rooms above the chow hall for the night.

Next morning Doc Blazer told us Roberts was dead. Said he'd been scalped.

"Scalped? Who'd want that carrottop?" Henry said. "Mescaleros?"

"Mescaleros won't touch the dead. Taboo."

A few of the boys dug a double grave in the old cemetery up the hill behind Doc Blazer's house. Doc's old carpenter made a double box, big enough for Dick and Roberts. It was a fine piece of joinery, not some rough-hewn crate. He lined it with white muslin. That afternoon Doc's daughter read the service.

I wasn't happy with Dick and Roberts tucked away for eternity in the same box. It would of been better if Dick instead of Charlie had shot Roberts. I reckon their fates were entwined. Much as I hated Roberts for being in Morton's posse, for hunting us like coyotes, most of all for killing Dick, I admired the old boy. He'd put up one hell of a fight. He got the best of us. He did for a fact.

CHAPTER 6 **MacNab**

No school today. Great danger rests on the town. God save us.

—DR. TAYLOR F. EALY, *Diary*, MAY 1, 1878

WITH DICK BREWER DEAD FRANK MacNab became our new leader. Charlie Bowdre was oldest and wanted the job, but he was an ornery maverick bull. Hadn't been for him Dick might still of been with us instead of sharing a box with Buckshot Roberts.

A few days after Blazer's Mill Judge Bristol rode into Lincoln to convene a grand jury. I was called again as a witness to John Tunstall's murder. There was a warrant out for me so I hid out the whole time. The grand jury indicted me and some of the boys for killing Brady and Hindman and Buckshot Roberts. Jesse Evans and a couple of other Dolan boys were indicted for killing John. Dolan was named an accessory, and him and Murphy were indicted for stealing John Chisum's cattle. I wasn't concerned about my indictments. Just glad to see Dolan and his boys get theirs. I was glad to hear about Mac McSween too. The grand jury said Mac didn't steal the Fritz estate. You recall that was the fracas that sent Morton's posse to confiscate John's livestock and murder him. The grand jury did everything but issue Mac an outright apology. That was a surprise. We'd figured Mac'd be indicted. Judge Bristol did too. Boys who witnessed the indictments said the judge did his damnedest to get the grand jury to change its mind.

While in Lincoln, Bristol appointed a new sheriff. The boy was from Kentucky. Owned a ranch south of Lincoln. We didn't know much about him. Figured he was in cahoots with Murphy and Dolan.

Word of the indictments got out quick. With so many of them, some of the Seven Rivers boys figured the new sheriff had more than he could handle. They formed a posse to round up Regulators. Wanted to help out, they said. They'd already begun combing Lincoln County.

Mac was meeting with Regulators in Uncle Ike Ellis's store when the mail carrier arrived from Roswell. He said Frank Coe and Frank MacNab were dead, shot near Roswell by Seven Rivers boys. Killers were headed to Lincoln, would arrive soon. Frank Coe was George Coe's cousin. Believe I told you that earlier.

"Goddam sumbitches!" George roared. "Them cabróns'll rue the day they crossed the Coe family."

He grabbed his Sharps and headed for the roof about the time the posse was entering the tunnel of trees at the near end of town. When the lead rider came into view, George fired. The slug from his rifle ripped through the cowboy's leg and creased his horse. The horse bucked, tossing the rider on his head. George measured the distance later. Said it was over four hundred paces. Near a quarter of a mile. A lucky shot if there ever was one. George is best I've seen with a rifle, but he ain't that good.

At the sound of gunfire the Regulators broke out of Ellis's store into the street. Lead was buzzing in both directions. Some of the posse raced up Main Street. They were the next casualties. The rest abandoned their horses and hunted for cover.

The sheriff stumbled out of Dolan's saloon. His foot missed the stirrup as he was mounting his horse. The horse spun in circles while he tried mounting again. When he finally got into the saddle he near fell off the backside.

"Where's that sidewinder heading?" I said.

"Believe he's hightailing," Fred Waite said. "He was drunk afore he got to Dolan's. Ain't sobered since. Probably prejudiced toward lead."

The sheriff whipped his horse and headed toward Fort Stanton. I considered spurring him along but saved my ammunition for the action at the other end of town.

We kept up steady fire but no one else was hit. An hour or two later a troop of buffalo soldiers rode in to the tune of "When Johnny Comes Marching Home." The sheriff wasn't with them. Figured he was sobering up at the fort. The shooting stopped as the troopers rode along Main Street.

"Ain't sure where this trail's headed," Fred said, "but I don't care for it. Too many warrants have our names on 'em. Vámonos, amigo."

"Bueno."

Fred and me ducked behind a wall until the troopers passed. We worked our way back to Ellis's store. George Coe was still on the roof.

"We ain't sticking around for the fandango," I called up to him. "Come with us."

"Can't do it, Billy. Ain't leaving till I find out where Frank's at. Sumbitches left him in a ditch somewheres. I aim to bring him home. No buffalo soldier'll keep me from burying my cousin."

"Entiendo. I was friend to Frank but not enough to swing from a rope."

"Don't concern yourself none, Billy. I'll be alright."

Fred and me went into Ellis's store. Uncle Ike was sitting in a rocking chair by the fireplace. Near as I could tell, he hadn't moved since the shooting started.

"Sorry for the ruckus, sir," I said. "We're passing through to our horses. Hoping not to get shot."

"Don't give it no nevermind, son. You boys are welcome anytime. Dolan and his boys are bad hombres. Bad for the town. 'Preciate what you done. Lots a folks feels the same."

Fred and me scooted out the back and lit out for San Patricio. We counted on the community protecting us. So far we'd been right. We'd already spent a fair amount of time in San Patricio but news of our whereabouts was so lean that none of Dolan's hombres'd looked for us there.

A few days later George and Frank Coe showed up with a few other

Regulators. Fred and me were knocking down stick pigeons back of Manuel Montoya's choza. Manuel was out in the field and his wife María was looking after a neighbor lady suffering from consumption.

"What the hell! Frank? George swore he'd pull you out of a ditch but I didn't expect a rabbit trick."

"Tweren't no trick," Frank said as he tied his horse to a rail in front of the choza. "When you boys started shooting, them Seven Rivers hombres took to the trees like turkeys. I was bringing up the rear. Hightailed it outta there."

"Mail carrier said you and MacNab were dead."

I holstered my six-shooter and walked over to shake Frank's hand.

"Glad he was wrong."

"He was right about MacNab. Killed straight out. I made a break for it. They shot my horse. Would of shot me cept they thought I's you, Billy. Figure that saved my life."

Frank and me and Fred Waite walked around the back of the choza and entered the kitchen while the rest of the boys hitched their horses. Frank and Fred settled in while I made coffee. The boys came in with Manuel who'd just finished his chores.

"Hey, Manuel," George Coe said. "Thanks for looking after these peckerwoods."

George turned to me and Fred.

"You boys skedaddled too soon," he said.

"How's that?"

"Mac went out to meet the soldiers. Told 'em what happened. The lieutenant thanked him, rounded up the Seven Rivers boys, and herded 'em to Fort Stanton. Ignored us Regulators. I watched the whole thing from Uncle Ike's roof. The lieutenant said nary a word as he passed by. Must of seen me. I know he heard me cause I cussed the lot of 'em. Manuel Segovia hollered at me, saying Frank weren't hurt. Only MacNab. Took credit for killing MacNab hisself. MacNab's horse with MacNab strapped to it was at the back of the parade. Mac pulled the horse out of line. Yesterday Frank showed up as we was putting MacNab in the ground."

There weren't enough chairs for everyone in the kitchen. George and Doc Scurlock were standing along the wall when I handed them their coffee.

"We elected Doc captain," George said.

"Congratulations," I said, shaking Scurlock's hand. "I reckon they're in order."

"Maybe not," Fred said. "Being captain weren't too rewarding for MacNab or Brewer. I hear the pay ain't all that great neither."

"It's a war for sure," Doc said. "Don't matter who you are. If you're a Regulator your chances of being killed are about the same. We've lost two boys, but not because they were captains. They were in the line of fire is all. When the killing stops let's hope they's more of us than them standing."

"Buena suerte, amigo," Fred said, raising his cup. "Now that the federales have put irons on the Dolan lot, is the law leaning our way?"

"Don't count on it," Doc said. "We got a break this week, but I'll bet my Winchester that when this war comes to a head, the army'll be on Dolan's side. The family of skunks has growed some. Manuel Segovia claims he killed MacNab. I believe him. He's moved to the head of my list. You boys care to help run down the little sonofabitch?"

"Hell yes," I said.

We flushed down our coffee, and me and Fred Waite collected our bedrolls and war bags. Fred brought the horses around while I thanked Manuel for his hospitality. I'd hoped María would return before we left but she didn't. A few minutes later we were heading back to Lincoln with the Regulators.

When we got to the Lincoln Road we ran into a detail of buffalo soldiers. The lieutenant said we were under arrest.

"What for?" Doc Scurlock asked.

"Assault and battery with intent to kill," the lieutenant said. "You boys shot up Lincoln a few days ago, in case you forgot."

"We was defending ourselves," Doc said. "Them boys come busting in after killing Frank MacNab. What'd you expect us to do? Let 'em round us up and hang us?"

"The Seven Rivers bunch is locked up," the lieutenant said. "But I've heard a different story from some of the folks in Lincoln. You boys are looking guiltier now than you did a few days ago. I'm putting you up at Fort Stanton until we get things sorted out."

"Folks in Lincoln, my ass," Doc said. "You mean Jimmy Dolan."

Doc was angry, but I figured the lieutenant was handing us a gift. Manuel Segovia should still have been at the fort.

"It's too pretty a day to argue, boys," I said. "Field larks are singing. There's nary a cloud in the sky."

I rode up to the lieutenant. The rest of the boys stayed where they were. The buffalo soldiers spread out around us, their rifles across their pommels.

"Come on, amigos. Let's ride with the boys in blue."

Doc rode up beside me. The rest of the boys bunched in behind.

"I don't hear no larks," he said.

When we arrived at the fort the lieutenant put us in one of the storage buildings. The Seven Rivers boys were in the guardhouse. On the second day the lieutenant let everyone out. We were confined to the fort but could move about as long as we stayed out of each other's way and avoided fights.

We'd planned an accident for Manuel Segovia but he wasn't around. He'd been rounded up with everyone else but he never showed at the fort. How he got away I never heard.

A couple of days later the sheriff sprung us. When we got back to Lincoln he made Doc Scurlock a deputy. Turns out we'd misjudged the new sheriff. He wasn't a Murphy man at all. He'd failed to mention that to Judge Bristol when he took the job. I was glad I hadn't shot him. Unfortunately, his tenure was brief. Making Doc a deputy was his undoing. When the governor learned the sheriff wasn't a Murphy man he fired him. Doc too. Put a Dolan lieutenant in his place.

In the meantime, while Doc was deputy, we were back on the side of the law. We had old warrants for some of the Seven Rivers boys and got a fresh warrant for Manuel Segovia.

A few days later a dozen of us rode to Dolan's cow camp on the Black River, hoping to find some Seven Rivers boys. Heard they'd stole MacNab's horses on the way home from Fort Stanton. If we were lucky, Segovia might be among them.

We spent the night in the hills overlooking the cow camp. Charlie Bowdre slipped down to the camp after dark. He reported back that three men were sleeping by a fire near the corral. Couldn't tell who they were. Several horses were in the corral. He didn't see anyone else.

Next morning when we rode up to the corral someone shot at us. Charlie and me jumped from our horses and ran for the corral. Scattered fire was coming in. I couldn't tell from where. Charlie looked through the fence at the horses.

"MacNab's," he said.

"Tunstall's too," I said.

Someone was creeping along the fence on the far side of the corral. Charlie raised his Winchester and fired.

"Got the sumbitch," he said.

Two men broke through the brush and disappeared into the tule along the river. The firing stopped. We waited. Nothing. None of us were hurt.

Charlie and me slowly worked our way around the corral. Whoever Charlie shot might still be alive.

"I'll be damned," Charlie said a moment later. "It's the turdhead hisself."

Segovia was lying beside the fence, blood oozing through his vest. His six-shooter in the dirt.

Charlie smashed the stock end of his Winchester against Segovia's head. It cracked like a walnut. Blood splattered my boots.

"What'll we do with this cabrón?" Charlie said when Doc showed up.

"Damn, Charlie! What'd you do that for?"

"Felt like it," he said.

"We can't take him back to Lincoln. God, he smells like a vinegarroon. Plant him here. You bring your shovel, Billy?"

I seemed to get the shit details. My age I reckon. Got my shovel and hunted up some soft loam near the river. After I dug the grave, Charlie helped me carry Segovia and put him in the ground. I covered him with dirt while Charlie collected river rocks to cover the grave and keep out varmints. A spring flood could carry him off but that'd be no concern of ours.

Next day we headed to Lincoln trailing MacNab and Tunstall stock. MacNab didn't have family and John had none this side of the Atlantic. Mac would sort it out.

CHAPTER 7 Cullins

Affairs in Lincoln have become serious, seeming approaching a crisis. The town is at the present writing in a perfect state of war.

—COL. NATHAN A. DUDLEY, LETTER TO COL. EDWARD HATCH, JULY 16, 1878

AS THE SUMMER HEATED UP, nerves were tight as barbwire. President Hayes said Lincoln's Main Street was the most dangerous street in the country. He sent a lawyer from New York to unravel the mess. Frank Angel was the lawyer's name. Mac said that Angel was looking for the cause of the troubles. He was especially interested in the governor and Judge Bristol.

Mac had been on the run for months. He was Dolan's hoodoo after John was murdered. Word was out that Dolan had put a fine price on him. Whenever a skirmish went sour, Dolan pressed the sheriff to dredge up a warrant with Mac's name on it. I didn't pay much attention to warrants. Knew I could skedaddle if anyone looked at me crosswise. But being a lawyer, Mac took warrants serious. He hid for a while at the Chisum Ranch. By mid-July he was tired of running. He holed up at home in Lincoln with a dozen of us.

Dolan had boys stationed in the torreón to the east of us and the Wortley Hotel to the west. Regulators began arriving in groups of half a dozen or more, taking up positions at Ellis's and Montaño's and Patrón's stores east of the torreón. Within a few days we had Dolan's boys outgunned. We took turns as lookouts on Mac's roof. The morning before the first shots were fired, Buck Powell's boys rode into town from the west and stopped off at the Wortley to confab with Dolan. An hour or two later shots smashed the shuttered windows on the west side of Mac's house. The siege was on.

Regulators and Dolan's hombres on the street took shelter wherever they could. Folks with no part in the battle ducked into houses and stayed there. We had sharpshooters on top of Montaño's store. They had clear views in both directions on Main Street and made sure no one moved against Mac's position.

Mac's shutters were soon shattered by gunfire. Mac had a stack of adobe bricks in the corral. Me and Kid Antrim brought back several armloads. We stacked the bricks in the windows, leaving enough daylight for gun placements and sightlines. Several of the boys dug portholes in the adobe walls. We had plenty of ammunition and figured we could hold off an army if it didn't have cannons.

We'd also laid in a couple of weeks' supply of food. During much of the day Sue and her sister Elizabeth cooked in the kitchen. Elizabeth's little daughter Minnie helped out. The gun battle occupied the front rooms of the house, so the women were safe. Boys wandered into the kitchen to eat whenever they were hungry or sought relief from the fighting. No one'd been hit except by flying glass. But flying lead had come close enough to remind us of our mortality.

When evening set in, the shooting quieted. Kid Antrim stood watch while the rest of us filed into the kitchen. Sue'd laid out as good a spread as I'd ever seen. Fried corn, okra, green beans, pork chops. The women had baked potatoes, squash, cornbread, and apple and egg-custard pies.

The boys were bumping shoulders, elbowing one another as they moved around the kitchen table, ladling food onto fine Kansas City plates with flowers painted on them. Most of the boys'd never seen such china. Crystal too. Sue said the crystal cups and bowls came from Ireland.

"You ladies outdone yourselves," Tom Cullins said. "If this is my last meal I'm heaven bound."

Cullins had been one of the first boys to sign up with the Regulators.

I didn't know much about him. A big man, head and a half taller than me, rawboned and strong. I seen him snatch an anvil from the ground once when I could barely tip it over.

"Thank you, Tom," Sue said. "Let's hold off heaven for a while. I want to see you boys get out of here alive."

The kitchen was too crowded to hold all of us. As the first of us filled our plates we went back to the parlor and sat on the floor, backs to the walls, plates in our laps.

"You think this battle could grow into a real war?" Cullins asked Mac.

"Anything's possible. But it seems unlikely. We're a backwater squabble to the rest of the nation. Why do you ask?"

"I was thinking about my pa. He fought in the war. Was killed at Shiloh. We didn't have no slaves. I reckon we was too poor. But Pap thought a man should stand up for what he believes. He believed in the Confederacy. I was wondering what he'd make of us warring against Dolan's boys because we believe in John Tunstall."

"I think he'd be proud of you, Tom."

"I can't see this being more than a range war," Rob Widenmann said. "If anybody's gonna start a real war in New Mexico, it's the greasers."

"Why them?" Mac asked.

"They hate us. I don't blame 'em. I was a kid when my folks left Coahuila, but I remember what it was like. I ain't Mex. But if I was, I'd hate us too. I'd talk up revolution ever chance I got."

"Hey, José," I said. "Widenmann says Mexicanos hate Americanos. Do you hate us?"

"Only if your polla is bigger than mine, pendejo."

"You're thinking like an American, Rob," Mac said. "If you were Mexican, you'd be a campesino tilling your half-acre. You'd be too poor to talk about revolution. You wouldn't be less of a person than you are today, but your concerns would mostly center around the weather, the crops, and the neighbors."

"If I was in trouble or hungry or needed a bed for the night," I said, "I don't know a campesino who wouldn't help. But if I was starving in Santa Fe there ain't a politician or businessman or lawyer who'd offer me a crumb. No offense, Mac."

"None taken. You're mostly right. People in power value wealth. They're reluctant to share. But there are a few rare coins who value some things more than money. John Tunstall was one."

"Hold on a minute, Mac," Widenmann said. "You saying greasers ain't inferior?"

"No they aren't inferior. We have the upper hand. That's all."

"They ain't as smart as us."

"Rob! Sure they are. If you could measure it you'd find some smarter, some dumber. Americans are better educated. That's all. Someone who lacks schooling may be ignorant. That doesn't mean he's dumb."

"I'll put my brain up against your chilito any day, cabrón," José said.

"You picked the wrong company to vent your opinion, Rob," Mac said. "José's smart. The smartest man in the room I'd wager. Also the fastest gun and the best shot. You may want to reconsider your words. His cousin Pedro was the smartest man I ever knew. He was a campesino. He couldn't read, but he could solve any problem. He'd have four solutions while the next man was wondering what the problem was."

"Don't know him."

"Too bad. He was one of the early casualties of Dolan's predations. He would have been an education for you. If you'd played monte with him you'd swear he'd marked the deck and knew where every card was. He never forgot anything. If you took him into the mountains to someplace he'd never seen he could lead you to the same spot a year later. He'd know where every stream was and how far away it was. He could see it all in his head. Read it back like it was a book he'd memorized. He told me once he thought in pictures, not words. An incredible memory. Every really smart man I've ever known had a fine memory. Like Billy's. Challenge him to a game of monte and see how you fare."

"I can repeat every dumbass thing you said last week, Widenmann," I said. "Want to hear?"

"You could say most anything and I wouldn't know if you was making it up."

"We all make do with what we have," Mac said.

"You make up for your poor memory with your pretty face, Widenmann," I said.

"You're the one with the pretty face. All them señoritas eying you. You oughta get some of them tintypes made. Pass 'em around."

"You boys are so sugary my sweet tooth's aching," Cullins said. "Believe I'll have another piece of pie."

Cullins was seated on the floor below a window. The window was shuttered and bricked, but much of the barricading had been blown away by gunfire. As he stood up, the crack of a Sharps came from the direction of the Wortley Hotel. Cullins fell to the floor. Half his head was missing.

"¡Puta madre!" José said. "¡Madre de Dios!"

"Jesus!" Mac said. "Oh god!"

Kid was still on guard duty. He shoved his Winchester through the window and sprayed half a dozen rounds in an arc down the street toward the hotel. We heard no return fire. Cullins was our first casualty.

Brains and blood'd splattered across the floor, raining on boots and bedrolls. I didn't favor cleaning it up. I figured me and Yginio Salazar were the youngest and most likely for the job so I nodded to him. I grabbed Cullins' shoulders and Salazar grabbed his feet. We hauled him through the kitchen on the Shields' side of the house so's not to upset the ladies. After checking for ambushers in the willows beside the Río Bonito we went out the back. We laid Cullins on the plaza between the wings of the house. We'd move him to the stable after dark.

When we got back to the parlor others were picking up pieces of skull and mopping the floor. Kid was cussing hisself.

"I should of seen him. He saw Cullins."

"He didn't see Cullins," I said. "It was dumbass luck. You couldn't of seen him if you were staring at him."

But I was talking to the breeze.

The good humor in the room was gone. No one said much the rest of the evening. After dark, Salazar and me went out the back to move Cullins to the stable. Kid came with us.

We told Mac we'd keep watch in case someone snuck up during the night. I volunteered for the first watch. That gave me time to think. Didn't know where this battle was headed but Mac wouldn't be much help. Someone had to take charge.

We'd laid our bedrolls between the house and the stable. When the moon rose high enough to flood the bedrolls I went over to Kid to wake him for the second watch. He was already awake. Salazar and me moved our bedrolls into the shadows and laid down again. We passed the night in quiet. When I awoke at first light Kid was sitting up. Salazar was still asleep.

Sue came out of the kitchen with a bucket, headed for the Bonito.

"I've got Arbuckle's on the stove if anyone's interested," she said.

"You're an angel, Miz Sue," Kid said. "I've been drinking boiled sagebrush since I run into Billy."

"Sagebrush? I reckon you don't like my biscuits either," I said.

"Biscuits, Billy?" Sue said. "Would you bake some for us?"

"Be happy to."

"Wonderful. The stove's hot. Oh, and there's a keg of gunpowder in the stable. Mac's afraid Dolan's men may steal it. Would one of you boys bring it to the house?"

"I'll get it, ma'am," I said, "but won't it be a hazard inside?"

"Mac says put it in the wardrobe in the bedroom. It should be okay there."

I washed up then went to the stable and got the gunpowder. Town was quiet. Elizabeth and Minnie were working in the kitchen when I came back. I set the keg in Mac's wardrobe. Mac was still asleep. Bodies littering the parlor floor leaned against one another like hogs at a trough. Some were groaning. Some were snoring. A hard day lay ahead.

CHAPTER 8 McSween

If it is within your power to loan me one of your howitzers,
I am of the opinion that parties for whom I have warrants
would surrender without a shot being fired.

—SHERIFF GEORGE W. PEPPIN, LETTER TO COL. NATHAN DUDLEY,
JULY 16, 1878

THE SECOND DAY WAS MUCH like the first. Gunfire and smoke, but no casualties. Acrid air hung over the town. Some of the boys had coughing fits. In the afternoon a couple of deputy sheriffs pounded on Mac's door.

"Open up, McSween. We got a warrant for your arrest. Warrants for Brown and Bonney too."

As Mac opened the door he said, "And we have warrants for your men."

"Show me your warrants," one of the deputies said.

"They're in our guns, cocksuckers," Rob Widenmann yelled across the room.

"Our warrants came from the justice of the peace," Mac said. "Your warrants from Judge Bristol are worthless. If they aren't void already they will be shortly. Have you talked to Frank Angel? He's the lawyer Washington sent to investigate this travesty. He assures me that the governor and Judge Bristol are being removed. He says the governor's administration is responsible for more corruption, fraud, and murder than any administration in the history of the United States. Of course, if you gentlemen want to step inside you can serve your warrants. I'm sure the boys will be accommodating."

"Let's go, Jack," the deputy said. "I knew this was a waste of time."

As the deputies headed toward the Wortley Hotel they kept looking over their shoulders until they were out of sight.

"Cocksucker?" one of the boys asked.

"Heard it from a kid in Santa Fe," Widenmann said.

Late that afternoon a buffalo soldier rode up Main Street. Someone fired at him from close range. A warning shot. Either that or the shooter couldn't hit a house if he was in it. Next day Dudley sent a detail into town to ferret out the shooter. They stopped at Mac's door.

"We've got company," Kid said. "That captain from the fort. He's horn-mad. Should I let him in?"

"I'll talk to him outside," Mac said as he opened the door.

"Good afternoon, Captain. What can I do for you?"

"Mr. McSween, I'm Captain George Purington, Ninth Cavalry, Fort Stanton. Yesterday your sheriff sent a letter to the commanding officer at Fort Stanton. He asked to borrow a howitzer to defend himself and his men. You may know, sir, that Congress last month passed the Posse Comitatus Act forbidding the United States Army from interfering in civilian matters. The commander had no choice but to deny the request. Last evening one of my troopers rode into Lincoln to deliver the commander's answer. While he was riding up Main Street, one of your men fired upon him. Fortunately he was not hit and he was able to deliver his message. Who shot at the trooper, sir?"

"No idea, Captain. All I can tell you is that it wasn't one of my men."

"Don't you have men at some of these other buildings?"

"I do."

"Then how can you be so sure?"

"Captain, I can speak only for the men in my house. But if any of my men from any building shot at one of your men, that trooper wouldn't be here today. Besides, we have no fight with the United States Army, and we don't want to start one. Why would we fire on a trooper?"

"He brought back a letter saying one of your men did it."

"Ah, the letter came from the sheriff or James Dolan. Am I right?"

"The sheriff."

"Okay then. If you're looking for someone who would fire at close range and intentionally miss a trooper riding through town, you can report to your commander that the shooter was one of Dolan's men. Dolan wants you in this tempest, and he wants you on his side. Preferably with your howitzer."

"Ever the lawyer aren't you, McSween. My man said he thought it was one of your men."

"He didn't see the shooter though did he. I'll bet he knew the contents of the sheriff's letter too. But, of course, that didn't influence his thinking. Good day, sir."

The captain started to say something but spun round and marched back to the street. He spoke to a buffalo soldier then mounted his horse. The soldiers jerked their horses around and cantered back toward Fort Stanton. The buffalo soldier who was bringing up the rear watched us until the detail passed the Wortley Hotel. That was the last we heard of the affair.

Not much happened the next couple of days. We exchanged fire but no one was hit. Of an evening after supper Sue played the piano. Kid and me joined in on cowboy favorites like "Streets of Laredo" and "Goodbye, Old Paint."

"This is no morgue, señora," José Chavez said one evening. "Billy and Kid know only grave songs. Can you play 'Cielito Lindo'?"

Sue complied and played a bouncy version. José and his cousin sang the verses. Kid and me chimed in on the chorus.

Ay, ay, ay, ay,
Canta, no llores,
Porque cantando se alegran,
Cielito lindo, los corazones.

José was right. After Sue quit playing we could hear Mexicans from Montaño's singing well into the night.

While we were eating dinner on the fourth day Henry Brown asked Sue about her life before Mac and her came to Lincoln.

"Billy says you grew up in Gettysburg, Miz Sue. I figure you was too young to remember the battle."

"You're a sweet boy, Henry, but I remember it alright," Sue said. "I lost my best friend. A beautiful bay with a white mane and tail. My grandfather had given her to me."

"What happened?"

"Confederate raiders took her. They showed up a couple of days before the battle. Daddy saw them coming and told me to take the horses to a cave below the barn. Mother fixed the soldiers a big breakfast. While they were eating one of their horses whinnied. Ours answered. When the soldiers left they took ours."

"My pap was there but he'd never talk about it. What was it like?"

"We lived a couple of miles from Culp's Hill, where the worst of the fighting was. Stray bullets broke windows in the farmhouse. We hardly slept. I'd pop up in bed if I heard a board creak. The last day was a deluge. It was the Fourth of July. The soldiers wanted to go home. Toward the end of the day they did. It was all so pointless. Eight thousand men died. The stench afterward was horrible. Bodies were barely buried. Dogs dug them up. A week after the battle my beagle brought home the cannon bone of a horse. Most of the meat still attached. I left home a few weeks later. My brother said bones turned up in the fields for years."

"You must of been skeered."

Sue didn't answer. She was looking at Cullins' bloodstain on the floor.

"You were skeered weren't you?"

"Not as bad as this."

Sue'd seemed in good spirits most of the time. She joked with the boys over meals and she enjoyed playing the piano of an evening, but maybe she was crumbling under the strain. The mood among most of the boys was good. We had Dolan's boys outnumbered. We had enough food and ammunition to hold off a siege. Mac was the real problem. He couldn't see an end to it. He couldn't stop whining.

"What happens when we run out of supplies? Dolan has an open supply route. He can hold us off for weeks. Months. Years even."

"It won't come to that," I said.

"What if it does?"

I respected Mac but he was wearing on me. Affecting the boys too. He took to praying out loud at night. Don't get me wrong, amigo. I got nothing against prayer. But out loud when boys are trying to sleep?

Long about noon the fifth day the Fort Stanton commander marched up Main Street with thirty or forty troopers and a howitzer and a Gatling gun. Dolan's boys took advantage of the disruption to improve their positions. Some moved into the Sisneros house across the street. Another group moved into Mac's stable, closing off our retreat.

The commander said he was there to protect women and children, but he aimed the howitzer at Montaño's and the Gatling gun at Mac's. He told his troopers to shoot anyone who fired at them. Over the next hour compañeros slipped out the back of Montaño's and disappeared into the cornfield.

It was quiet most of the afternoon. We weren't willing to open fire with the Gatling gun bearing on us. I figured Dolan's boys weren't either until a black flag appeared on the Wortley Hotel. When Mac saw the flag he wrote a note to the commander. He asked me to read it to the boys.

> General, sir. Would you have the kindness to tell me why soldiers surround my house? Before blowing up my property I would like to know the reason. The constable is here and has warrants for the arrest of the sheriff and posse for murder and larceny. Respectfully, A. A. McSween.

"Sounds good," I said. "The commander's no general, but no harm calling him one."

Mac handed the note to his niece Minnie.

"Honey, take this to the soldiers across the street. Tell them to give it to the general in charge."

Minnie was terrified.

"Hold on, Mac," I said. "Send one of the boys out. Send me."

"It's okay," Mac said. "Someone will shoot you. No one'll bother a little girl."

He turned to Minnie.

"You'll be safe, honey."

"You can say she's safe, Mac," I said. "But she don't know it."

Mac wasn't listening. He cracked the door for her to slip through.

"Don't run. Act normal and give it to the first soldier you see."

Minnie held back from the doorway, clutching a rag doll to her chest. Mac pulled a handkerchief from his pocket and gave it to her.

"Wave this over your head. It means you're coming in peace. No one will harm you."

"Baby Jesus, protect me," she said as she stuck her hand through the doorway, waving the handkerchief as hard as she could.

She hesitated a moment, then slipped outside. The street went quiet as she crossed it, waving her white flag overhead and holding the doll next to her face. The noise in the soldiers' camp ceased. The town went quiet. Mac opened the door wide so the boys could watch. Minnie walked up to the nearest trooper and handed him the note. She spoke to him, then turned and slowly walked back, still waving her little flag and clutching her doll.

When she came through the door the room erupted. Mac grabbed her in a bear hug. She grinned at the applause. Kid went into the kitchen to tell Elizabeth.

"My big brave beautiful little girl," Mac said.

Elizabeth ran into the parlor and yanked Minnie away.

"What have you done!"

Mac tried to explain but Elizabeth would hear none of it.

"You should be ashamed, asking a little girl to do what you're too cowardly to do. Don't ever risk my baby again."

Elizabeth pulled Minnie into the kitchen. Mac sank into a chair.

A short while later a trooper came across the street. Kid opened the door and the trooper handed him a note.

A. A. McSween, sir. I am directed by the Commanding Officer to inform you that no troops have surrounded your house and that he desires to hold no correspondence with you. He directed me to say that if you desire to blow up your house he has no objection, providing you do not injure any of his command by doing so.

Mac exploded. "Sonofabitch! Sonofabitch!"

That afternoon a pall hung over the parlor during supper. Mac looked low as a horntoad, his plate untouched.

"Whadda you think, Billy?" Kid said. "I was feeling good afore the army brought in them cannons. The boys have abandoned Montaño's. Should we clear out?"

"Won't be easy. Dolan's boys are watching the back door. Best chance is after dark before the moon is up."

About then Sue ran into the parlor crying, "Lord help us, the kitchen's on fire!"

Kid and me raced into the kitchen. Smoke was pouring over the top of the back door. Flames were licking the latillas.

"Water! Quick!"

Elizabeth pulled a pan from the stove and handed it to Kid. He threw the water onto the vigas. Flames guttered then flared again.

"More! We need more!"

"That's all we have!"

"They must of snuck up from the stable," Kid said. "We're in a snake pit now."

"Fire'll take the house," I said. "You ladies take the kids and leave. Now."

"I'm not leaving Mac," Sue said. "Elizabeth, you take the children and go."

"I won't go without you," Elizabeth said, and that was that.

Kid and me and some of the boys grabbed rugs, coats, anything at hand to beat back the flames. It was a losing proposition. The flames advanced overhead through the kitchen and into Mac and Sue's bedroom. We retreated from room to room as the ceilings gave way. When the burning latillas fell they set the floors on fire.

I'd forgotten about the keg of gunpowder in the wardrobe until it blew. The explosion ripped a hole into the plaza between the wings of the house. The whole town must of heard it. We'd abandoned the bedroom before it blew. No one was hurt.

"Sue, Elizabeth, you've got to get your family out of here," I said. "If the fire holds off we'll make a break for it after dark. There'll be gunfire for sure. If you leave now you can walk out in daylight. In safety. Do it for the kids."

"What about Mac?"

He was in a corner of the parlor, curled up like a baby.

"Mac'll come with us. If he leaves now he'll be shot for sure and you ladies'll be caught in the crossfire."

"Will you take care of him, Billy?"

"He'll be at my side."

"Bless you. Godspeed."

Sue hugged me and kissed me on the mouth. She went over to Mac and took his face in her hands and kissed him. He was crying. Kid opened the front door wide enough for the ladies to slip through. Sue stuck her arm out and waved a handkerchief. She stepped out the door. The street went quiet. Sue motioned to her sister. Elizabeth and the children walked out behind her, Minnie carrying her doll.

When the parlor ceiling began to burn, the smoke and heat forced us into the Shield side of the house. Falling embers turned Mac's library into an inferno. We were in the Shields' bedroom when Sue's piano exploded. Piano wires popped like a Gatling gun. The fire was moving faster. I figured we'd run out of rooms before we'd run out of daylight but I kept my concerns to myself.

It was dusk when we moved into the Shields' kitchen. We'd long since run out of things to fight the fire. We bided our time, waiting for the dark to clear a path to the river. We stayed in the house till our skin was near scorched.

"We wait much longer our gooses'll be cooked," I said. "We'll be easy targets getting out the door but the night'll swallow us. A few of you come with me. I'll make a break for the store. We'll keep Dolan's boys pinned down in the stable while the rest of you crawl along the wall. When you get to the coop, run for the gate."

"I'm with you, Billy," Kid said.

José Chavez and three others also volunteered.

"Druther you stay behind, Kid. Look after Mac. I promised Sue to keep him with me but he'll have a better chance with you."

The backyard was lit up but the Río Bonito was hidden in the night. Five of us burst through the back door, firing into the stable as we ran. Half a dozen steps out we met return fire. I zigzagged toward Tunstall's Store. One of the boys was in front of me when we reached the side gate between the house and the store. He was hit and he fell into the gate, knocking it open. I ran through it and into the store. The rest were right behind me. None of us was hit.

We hammered lead into the stable. The return fire subsided. In a minute or two Kid and Mac and the rest crawled out the back door along the adobe wall. Dolan's boys in the stable couldn't see them. Firing from the stable resumed but it was coming toward us. Mac must of figured the fire was raining down on him.

He stood up, waving his Bible, yelling, "I surrender! I surrender!"

A fusillade poured out of the stable. Mac fell backward. His legs twitched a couple of times then he was gone. The boys scrabbled toward the back gate. One of Dolan's hombres was waiting. When the boys reached him he killed the first one through the gate. Kid shot the hombre in the face and ran past.

Lead splintered the wood beside my head. A chunk hit me in the cheek. The shot came from behind me.

"¡Puta madre!" José said. "Soldados. Vámonos, muchachos."

A dozen men in the shadows were coming toward us. José and the rest ran toward the river. I broke for the willows and raced after them.

CHAPTER 9 **Olinger**

As a law-enforcing officer Bob Olinger was considerate and generous. . . . Bob was helpful to Mother. She thought very highly of him.

—LILY KLASNER, *My Girlhood among Outlaws*

KILLING MAC PRETTY MUCH ENDED the Lincoln County War. There were still some skirmishes, but with Tunstall and Mac dead there wasn't much left to war over. The Regulators, of course, still wanted justice for John's killers. Mac's too. The governor and his friends wanted the Regulators out of business. They hired Pat Garrett for the job. Over the next three years ten or fifteen hombres died on each side.

President Hayes fired the governor and appointed Lew Wallace in his place. Wallace offered amnesty to anyone in the war, hoping to put an end to the killing, but he was more interested in writing than running the territory. He resigned after publishing *Ben-Hur*, his big book about a Jew in Roman times betrayed by his best friend. It's a good story. Ben-Hur becomes a slave. When he earns his freedom he vows revenge. Then he meets Jesus. I won't tell you what happens. You may want to read it yourself. Your brother loved it. He mentions it in his diary.

I met Wallace once. A year after Mac died. He was no Ben-Hur. He promised me amnesty but he didn't honor it. He wanted me to testify against Jimmy Dolan and his boys for murdering the one-armed lawyer Sue hired after Mac's murder. I saw the whole thing. Dolan and his boys were drunk. They were so close to the old boy their six-shooters set his clothes afire.

Late in December, a couple of years after Mac died, Garrett and his boys ambushed a bunch of us in Fort Sumner. They killed one Regulator. The rest of us got away. Over the next few days we moved from ranch to ranch. On Christmas Eve we got caught in a bad snowstorm. We holed up for the night in the old Alejandro Perea place at Stinking Springs. The stone choza had a single doorway. No windows. The door'd been gone for years. Firewood probably.

The last visitor'd left a stack of firewood in a corner of the choza. I built a fire while the boys put up the horses and settled in for the night.

"If these logs don't last and the night gets as cold as I suspicion," I said, "we'll be lucky to make it till morning."

"They's worse ways to go than freezing to death," one of the boys said. "Drift off to sleep peaceful like. I could live with that."

"I know one kind of death I couldn't live with," Charlie said. "You hear what happened to Widenmann?"

"Rob? Dead?" I said. "What happened?"

"You know that bitch his pa keeps tied up back of the goat pen?"

"I hunted lions with her and Rob's uncle in the Sacramentos a while back. She's a fine girl."

"Rob thought so too. He tried to screw her."

"You're shitting me!"

"Wished I was. She clipped it clean off. Balls and all."

"¡Madre de Dios! He bleed out?"

"Afore he got to the house. They found him next morning facedown in the goat path, wearing nothing but a nightshirt."

When we awoke next morning Charlie was first out to take a piss. He was about my size and wore a broadbrim hat like mine. Garrett and his posse were waiting. Gunfire erupted. Charlie fell back through the doorway, leaking from a dozen holes. Our horses were hobbled outside. Kid coaxed Charlie's mule to the doorway only to have it riddled with bullets. It fell through the entrance, blocking our escape.

"That you, Pat?" I called.

"It's me, Billy. You and whoever else is in there, throw out your guns and come out. One at a time. Hands overhead."

"Pat, Pat, why would we do a fool thing like that?"

"Simple arithmetic, Billy. You were pretty good at it when you were rustling cattle. How many you got in there? Six? Five if you count the ones still alive. That's what five horses and a dead mule say. You got one exit. Blocked by a mule. Me, I got twenty guns pointed a foot above the mule and another ten round back. How's that add up?"

"Adds up to a lie, Pat. You ain't got thirty guns unless you carrying them yourself. You couldn't raise half a dozen hombres in this weather."

"Count the holes in your camarada."

"It ain't thirty."

"Who'd we kill? My boys got a little overanxious when he stepped into the doorway."

"Charlie Bowdre. You ain't got a warrant for him have you."

"He ain't complaining. If we shouldn't of shot him, come on out and plead his case. We'll parlay."

"Patience, Pat, patience. We've got cases for you. Brass cases. You'll have to wait for them though."

We spent the better part of the day strategizing. Doc Scurlock and Kid wanted to make a break for the horses. We couldn't see the horses and weren't rightly sure where they were. I figured they were already in Pat's custody. None of us thought Pat had more than a handful of hombres, but there were likely more of them than us. I wanted to wait for nightfall, see what we could learn about the posse in the meantime, then evaluate our chances. Two of the boys who didn't have warrants hanging over them were ready to throw out their guns.

"They'll starve us out," one of the boys said. "We ain't got grub. I near froze last night. Another night like that, I'll be stiff as cordwood."

It didn't help that Pat had a fire going. He'd built it upwind and laid on sweet-smelling chorizo and coffee.

"Hey, Pat," I called out. "We're gonna be here awhile. Send over a pot of coffee. Some of the boys' brains ain't working too good. Coffee'll grease them up. We'll get out of here quicker."

"I've got a fresh pot, Billy. Saving it for you. Thick as swamp water.

The way you like it. You boys come on out. We'll sit around the fire and drink some. Feed you eggs and chorizo too afore we leave. Warm you up. You'll feel better. Think better too."

"Kindly offer but we'd prefer our coffee in here."

"Can't do it, Billy. Coffee's conditional."

"Keep it hot. We'll think about it."

I continued bantering with Pat, asking about his food supply, was he warm enough, did he have enough oats and water for the horses. Anything to give us clues about his men. We'd hear occasional conversations around the back of the choza, but they were too muted to offer much counsel. By midafternoon, when Pat laid more meat on the fire, the two boys who wanted to quit earlier had had enough.

"Sorry, amigos," one of them said. "We're throwing in."

They tossed their hardware out the door.

"Hold up, Pat. We're coming out. Hope you ain't et all the grub."

We shook hands and they clambered over Charlie's mule.

"Sonofabitch," Doc said. "Whadda we do now?"

Kid and me argued for waiting till dark.

"We made it out of Mac's after dark," Kid said.

"Some of you didn't," Doc said. "Even if two make it, you want to be the third, laying here beside Charlie? Our best chance is to turn ourselves in. Lots can happen twixt now and the noose."

"You're too logical, Doc. You ain't thinking."

"You got a better idea?"

I didn't. By sundown him and Kid were ready to quit.

"I ain't going," I said. "You're too determined to get yourselves hung. Do me a favor. Let me know how many hombres are out there. I'll wait and see what the night brings."

We shook hands, then Doc called to Pat, "Kid and me are coming out. Don't shoot. Billy's mulling it over."

Doc and Kid held their rifles and six-shooters high and clambered over the mule.

In a few minutes Doc called out, "You lying sonofabitch! If we'd knowed you was only four we'd of made a break for it."

"If you had you'd be dead."

Pat was probably right. He'd hornswoggled us. Moving men around the back, talking in whispers, making us think there were more of them. I felt like a fool but I was glad I'd stayed.

"Come on out, Billy. You can't stay forever. It'll be cold again tonight. I won't leave without you. Your amigos left their bedrolls behind. If we wait till morning they'll be icicles. I'll have to haul 'em in on a travois."

"Don't give it another thought," I said as I tossed out the bedrolls.

Doc came over and picked them up.

Pat and his boys got to arguing. One of them wanted to take the four in hand and head for Santa Fe. I liked that option. Another wanted to storm the choza. I was okay with that too. In the end Pat decided to hunker down for the night and see how agreeable I'd be in the morning.

The temperature was falling fast. I shook out Charlie's bedroll to cover mine and pawed through his war bag looking for anything to keep me warm. I pulled out a scalp with red hair.

"¡Puta madre! Buckshot Roberts! Bowdre, you shit-eating peckerwood!"

I flung the war bag and scalp into the night.

A few hours after dark another snowstorm struck. Almost a blizzard, causing confusion in Pat's camp. Figured it was my chance. Probably my only chance. I'd already put on everything I could wear. I wrapped my blanket around me and grabbed my Winchester, then I crawled over the mule. The snow was blowing hard, a white wall blocking sounds. I made it out the door and crawled along the front wall low as a lizard. When I got to the corner I turned and clung along the sidewall toward the back of the choza. Heard muffled voices. When I reached the back wall I turned the corner again and crouched. Still nothing. No yelling. No shooting. I was about to run when I felt a jab in my side.

"Where you headed, Billy?"

Garrett's Winchester nuzzled my armpit.

"Hello, Pat. Stepping out for a piss. It's pretty rank in there."

"Come back round tother side. Piss wherever you like. But hand over your Winchester and six-shooter first. Be easy about it. I'd hate to have to shoot you. We've always been friends."

Garrett hauled me and the others to Santa Fe. Three months later I was in La Mesilla facing murder charges for killing Buckshot Roberts and Sheriff Brady. The Roberts bill said it was a federal case because Roberts was killed on the Mescalero Reservation. When my lawyer proved that the killing took place at Blazer's Mill, off the reservation, the judge dismissed the charge. The United States had no jurisdiction.

I wasn't so lucky with Brady. Was sentenced to hang. The fact that I never shot the sheriff made no difference. Not to the judge. Not to my lawyer. The lawyer who represented me in the Roberts case did a fine job. Albert Fountain was my lawyer in the Brady case. He never even talked to me. Dolan drummed up eyewitnesses who weren't never there. Fountain didn't bother to cross-examine them. Besides the shooters, there was only one witness still alive when Brady was killed. I tried to shoot him, and he did shoot me, but he was hightailing it down the street when Brady got hit. Couldn't of seen what happened. Dolan and his boys wanted me to hang. Brady was as good an excuse as any. The trial was over in a day and a half. The judge picked a day in May for the hanging. Friday the thirteenth, he said. He thought it was funny. Garrett put me in leg irons and shackled me in an ambulance. We left out late at night. Half a dozen marshals rode with us back to Lincoln. They figured I'd have friends waiting along the way.

By then Dolan was out of business. Too deep in debt. He sold out to lawyers from Santa Fe. They figured the old Murphy and Dolan store would make a dandy courthouse. Lincoln didn't have one and it was the county seat.

The calaboose was on the second floor. No cell. Just an open room. It had a table and three chairs and a cot. My leg irons were shackled to an iron ring bolted through the floor. I could walk in a circle or sit at the table or lie on the cot. That was my home for the next week. It was comfortable compared to the old pigsty under the sheriff's office. Jailers were two of Garrett's deputies, Bob Olinger and Jim Bell. Bell was okay. I felt bad about what happened to him. Olinger was different. He could rankle the dead. After Governor Wallace offered amnesty to anyone in the Lincoln War, one of the Regulators ran into Olinger in Dolan's saloon.

Offered to shake hands. No hard feelings. The ole boy stuck out his hand. Olinger took it but wouldn't turn loose. While the boy was trying to pull hisself free, Olinger shot him through the mouth. Witnesses said the Regulator drew first.

Olinger hated me. I'd bested him too many times at monte. He swore I was palming cards but I couldn't have done it if I'd wanted to. My hands were too small. If he couldn't recover his dinero he'd take it out of my hide. Time and again he baited me while I was in the calaboose but I wouldn't bite. Bided my time. He carried a Remington side-by-side shotgun. Ten-gauge. First breechloader I'd seen. He'd come close, taunting me, hoping I'd make a grab for the gun. I was no fool. Olinger had six inches and fifty pounds on me. To beat him the odds would have to be better. Considerably. One time he laid the shotgun on the floor within reach. He turned his back and walked to the window.

"Come on, Bob, you can do better'n that. That scatter-gun ain't loaded. You think I'm such a dumbass. You're dumber'n dog shit."

"I'll get you, you half-pint sumbitch. You can bet on that. You'll never see the rope. You won't live long enough."

"I'll take that bet. For a double eagle. I won't see the rope, but not because I won't live long enough."

Bob rushed at me, grabbing the shotgun as he came.

"I'll collect that bet now, with a double barrel 'stead of a double eagle."

He swung the shotgun. I wasn't fast enough in my leg irons. When I came to, Garrett was tongue-lashing him.

"You idjit. This ain't how we treat prisoners. You lay another hand on Bonney, I'll see you locked up till your grandkids are growed."

That was the last torment I had from Olinger. My head hurt for days but it was worth it. Stopped his badgering. Afterward Garrett had two deputies guarding me at all times.

On my last day Olinger left me alone with Bell while he went to the Wortley for dinner. Before he left he put the shotgun on the rack in the next room. I told Bell I had to go to the jakes. Bell cuffed me and walked me downstairs.

"You wiping my ass?" I said. "I can't do it with these cuffs."

"You'll figure a way."

I walked out the backdoor, leg irons jangling, Bell following. I went into the jakes and took a piss. When I came out Bell's six-shooter was leveled at me.

"You think I'd rush you with these irons?"

"You're a slippery weasel. Ain't taking no chances."

We started back up the stairs, Bell's six-shooter in my back. I can fold over my small hands so they're not much bigger than my wrists. I slipped out of the cuffs, then faked a fall on the top step, tripping over my leg irons. As I spun to the side I yanked the six-shooter from Bell. He was caught off guard and fell backward. When he looked up he was looking down the barrel of his six-shooter.

"Give me the key to the irons, Jim," I said. "I'll be on my way. No fuss, no blood."

"Pat has the only key."

Bell turned and looked down the stairs.

"Don't do it, Jim. I'd shoot Olinger soon as I'd shoot a sidewinder, but I got no truck with you."

Bell looked at me and hesitated, then he bolted down the stairs. I hesitated too. Didn't want to shoot him, but Olinger was out there and Bell would head straight for him. I fired twice. Bell tumbled down the stairs and crumpled to the floor.

I shuffled into the room where Olinger left his shotgun. I took it from the rack and checked the load, then shuffled to the window. Olinger must of heard the shots because he was racing across the street toward the jail. I leaned out the window.

"Hello, Bob."

He glanced up then stopped short, reaching for his six-shooter.

"You sum—"

I opened up his chest with both barrels. Double eagles, I said to myself. I reloaded, then blew apart the chain between my leg irons. A splinter from the floorboards leapt up and lodged in my gun hand. I plucked it out with my teeth, then I put Olinger's shotgun back on the rack. I went downstairs and out the front door carrying Bell's six-shooter. The shooting had cleared the street. My old compadre George Coe'd been on the street when I shot Olinger. I called out to him. He stepped out of the Wortley.

"Hey, George, can you fetch me the blacksmith?"

"Sure, Billy. Think he's in his shop."

I stepped back into the courthouse and waited until George returned with the blacksmith. He wasn't a Regulator but he was sympathetic. Mac'd bailed him out a couple of times when he'd been locked up for drunkenness. In a few minutes I was a free man.

About then the constable rode into town.

"Hey, amigo, I need to borrow your horse. You'll have him back afore nightfall."

I was still holding the six-shooter. The constable handed me the reins. Didn't say nothing. As I leapt on the horse he reared and tossed me on my back. I scrabbled from under his hooves and grabbed the reins.

"Steady, big boy. I promised your boss he'll see you soon."

He calmed down and we lit out for San Patricio. A couple of miles out of town I dismounted at Yginio Salazar's house. Salazar was home. I borrowed a horse. Aimed the constable's horse toward Lincoln and swatted his rump. Then I rode to María and Manuel Montoya's and holed up a few days while Garrett and his boys looked for me. No one'd seen me borrow Salazar's horse, so when Garrett saw it in San Patricio he didn't suspicion it.

Later I wished I'd kept Olinger's shotgun. It was beautiful. I've never seen another like it. At the time, though, I figured it would be a liability. It would be hard enough finding shells for it, and it would attract attention.

Couldn't believe he'd buffaloed me with it. Could of broke the stock, the dumbass.

Manuel got me another horse and returned Salazar's. He also got a rifle and provisions enough for me to hole up till things cooled down. I rode to Portales Springs and laid up for a month. Then I went looking for Kid. Garrett'd cut him loose after Stinking Springs since Kid had no warrant on his head. I found him in San Patricio. Him and me rode to Pima County in Arizona Territory. We were gone a couple of months.

I had a girl in Fort Sumner. Paulita Maxwell. Hadn't seen her in forever and I was getting lonesome. She was pregnant and I was the pa. Leastwise she said I was and I believed her.

"Paulita's swelled up like a toad," Kid said. "Can't give you nothing. They's plenty of señoritas here. Forget about Fort Sumner awhile."

"Need to check on her and my boy."

"What if it ain't a boy?"

"Then I'll love her like her momma."

We were a couple of weeks reaching Fort Sumner. We rode east across New Mexico, stopping in Silver City to see old haunts and visit Aunt Cat's grave. The site of my first theft was still there. A Chinese laundry. I'd stolen clothes. Just a dumbass kid, not more than fourteen. Got caught. We rode by the jail where I made my first escape. Up the chimney after dark. Got stuck part way up and panicked. Figured I'd be there next morning when the sheriff came in to build a fire. I could see my britches scorching, me scorching with them. Once I got my breathing back I scrabbled to the roof. I was covered with soot topping out and had a coughing fit. A couple of cowpokes on the street looked up, but I reckon I was black against the night sky. Stole a horse from a neighbor and lit out for Arizona. Ran into soldiers near the San Carlos Reservation. They had scouts with them. You may of been one of them. That was before I knew you.

The trip with Kid was the first time I'd been back to Silver City. We left there and rode to Dolan's cow camp on the Black River, looking for trouble. A couple of Mexicans were in the bunkhouse eating tortillas and beans when we arrived. We put blankets over our heads and busted in, firing six-shooters, roaring like the wrath of God. They dropped their suppers and ran for the river. We collected their hardware and saddles and chased off their horses. We couldn't use the saddles so we dropped them along the road as we left. Figured they'd find them in the morning. It was all in good sport. We were gratified anytime we could make mischief at Jimmy Dolan's expense.

We left the camp and headed north to John Chisum's ranch. Uncle John's niece Sallie was there. She was a sight. Pretty and smart and fun. Kid and me played croquet with her. She invited us to supper. Uncle John was out on the range for a couple of days. That was alright with me. He knew about my troubles and figured I was a bandido like Garrett said I was. Sallie and me'd been sweet on one another, even after I'd met Paulita. I hoped to take advantage of it while we were alone. It was a lot easier without Uncle John about.

I spent the night with her. Kid slept in the barn. Next morning we headed north to Fort Sumner.

CHAPTER 10 **Fort Sumner**

We had a game of poker together, and while we were playing, I told Billy the best thing he could do was to get up and be gone three or four years. Then he could come back and there would be nothing said or done about what happened in the Lincoln County War.

—PAT GARRETT, AS TOLD TO JOHN P. MEADOWS, DATE UNKNOWN

IT WAS EARLY JULY WHEN Kid Antrim and me rode into Fort Sumner. The army'd left shortly after the War between the States. Back then the community around the fort was called Sunnyside, but we called it all Fort Sumner. The fort. The town. That's what it's still called today.

We'd been holed up at the Yerby Ranch a few hours out of town, hoping things would quiet down. We knew Garrett was looking for me and he'd know I'd go to Fort Sumner to see Paulita. She lived with her brother, Pete Maxwell. Kid and me left the Yerby Ranch and rode to the Maxwells. We put up our horses in the corral. Pete saw us and came onto the porch.

"Billy! Hey, Paulita, Billy's here."

Pete and me shook hands.

"Garrett's looking for you. Was here two days ago. He'll be back. Could be this evening."

"Yeah, Pat wants to stretch my hide but I had to see Paulita."

"I thought you were here for the holiday."

"Holiday?"

"Le quatorze juillet. La fête nationale. Bastille Day."

"Sounds Frenchy."

"It is Frenchy. I'm half French you know."

"I missed the hoopla on the Fourth, Pete. Reckon I'll miss the fourteenth too."

"Not a chance. We're celebrating."

"How's Paulita?"

"Fine. Took her to the doc last week. The kid's fine too. Let's quit jawing out here. Come inside and cool down. You introducing me to your amigo?"

"This here's Kid Antrim. Kid, meet Pete Maxwell, son of the famous Lucien Maxwell, largest landowner in New Mexico Territory. Hell, for all I know, largest in the world."

Pete and Paulita lived in a big house that old Lucien bought from the army years before. It was a board-and-timber two-story house, not adobe like most in the territory. Full porches on four sides. It's gone now. Back then it was one of the biggest houses around.

"Always glad to meet a friend of Billy's," Pete said.

Paulita was coming out of the bedroom when we walked into the kitchen.

"Oh, Billy, Billy, Billy," she said as she rushed to me crying. "Sheriff Garrett's looking for you. If he finds you he'll shoot you sure . . . I'm so happy to see you."

"Don't worry none, Paulita," I said as I hugged her. "Pat ain't near as good a lawman as he thinks. I won't be here long. Wanted to see you and Little Billy."

"Little Billy! You may be right. The rascal kicks like a boy."

Kid and me spent the afternoon with Pete and Paulita. I'd like to of stayed the night but I worried that Pat might recognize our horses in Pete's corral. Figured my best move was to stay at Celsa Gutierrez's. Garrett's sister-in-law. The sisters were from Fort Sumner. They had other kin there too. All friends of mine. None of them cared much for Garrett. Wasn't sure how much Garrett's wife cared for him either. I didn't expect him to be showing up at Celsa's.

When we made our goodbyes I told Paulita I'd be back for her after I'd talked with Celsa. Kid and me went to Celsa's and put our horses in her corral. Celsa said we could stay the night in her parlor but we should be careful. By then I was so sleepy I could hardly stay awake. Celsa told me I could rest on her bed for a bit. I fell asleep and had another of my dreams about Aunt Cat. She was standing on the porch of a house I'd never seen. It was starting to rain and she was crying when I woke up.

When I came out of Celsa's bedroom Pete was in the kitchen.

"Garrett's back. Don't come to the house. I'll send Paulita after dark."

"Thanks, Pete. I'll stick around till morning, but I got to get out of here. For good. I didn't want to scare Paulita but Garrett's a skunk bear. If I stick around, my odds of seeing next year ain't all that favorable."

"Where you heading, Billy?" Kid asked.

He'd come in from the corral after feeding the horses. I was at the table with Pete. Kid sat across from me.

"You coming with me?"

"I'm surprised you'd ask."

"Can't go back to Texas. Too many conocidos. Old Mexico maybe. Or California."

"My father loved California," Pete said. "He was there with Kit Carson, scouting for John Frémont. Said it had everything. Ocean. Mountains. Deserts. Trees so big you could carve a hut out of the trunk. He thought it was paradise."

"California's got cities you could get lost in," Kid said. "A hundred thousand people live in San Francisco. You believe that? Saw it in the *New Mexican* last month. Paper showed a mule pulling a railcar up the street. We could be mule-train robbers."

"My outlaw days are over," I said. "Enjoyed it but it's time to grow up."

"Grow up? You know lots a growed outlaws. How you going to feed yourself?"

"I wasn't no outlaw working for John Tunstall. You weren't neither when you were working for the Coes. Me and you could work a ranch together. I could be a marshal in California. Like Garrett. I'm a fair cook. I cooked for a hotel in Arizona Territory a while back. I could play monte. Like Bill Hickok. Maybe earn enough to buy my own spread. There're lots I could do. But there's one thing I won't do no more. Outlawing."

"Sure. Be like Hickok," Pete said. "Face down on a poker table with a bullet in your back."

"I'll tell you, boys, I've a better chance catching a bullet as an outlaw than as a gambler. Besides, from what I hear it wasn't poker that brought Hickok down. Jack McCall said he was avenging his brother."

Didn't want to say anything to Pete and Kid, especially after Kid said he'd go with me, but I'd been considering Tombstone in Arizona Territory. Doc Holliday was there. I'd run into him in a card game a few months earlier. He said Wyatt Earp was in Tombstone. Earp said the town was sitting on a silver strike bigger than the Comstock lode. Grubbers were making fortunes, gamblers even more. I could play monte. But grubbing for silver was the bigger attraction. I could disappear for months in the Mules. No one'd know I was there. It's beautiful country. I was there once when I was working in Arizona. The time I ran into you and Tom Horn on the San Carlos. But I figured Pete or Kid would laugh at me being a grubber. Besides, Kid probably wouldn't go with me to Tombstone. He hated Chiricahua country. Gerónimo plum terrified him.

Pete suggested I head up the Río Chama.

"There's a small mission half a day's ride from Abiquiu," he said. "If it's still there. Black Monks."

"You mean like buffalo soldiers?"

"No. Monks wearing black robes. But they're not Black Robes. They're called Black Monks. Like hermits. Hardly anybody knows the place. You could hide out there till you get your bearings."

"Black Monks. Never heard of them."

"They'd been on the Chama a year or two when I met them. Living in jacales. Planning on building a church. Jicarillas helped them. Showed them how to garden. Supplied them with game."

The idea of hermits living in the desert surrounded by hostiles sounded crazy. After the Comanches killed my ma and pa I went to live with Aunt Cat. She brought me up Catholic. I knew Black Robes were Jesuits. Black Monks were a mystery.

"How'd you know about them," I asked.

"Ran into them when I was in the military under Kit Carson. Beginning of the Long Walk campaign. We were rounding up Indians, Navajo mostly, moving them here. I was with a detail hunting strays on the Río Chama when we found the monks. Stayed with them a few days."

"I heard the Injuns didn't stay long," Kid said.

"Carson knew more about Navajos than his commanders did. They couldn't grow crops. They were herders, not farmers. The military finally turned them loose and shut down the fort. A couple of years later Pap bought the buildings. This house was officers' quarters. Our stable was the old quartermaster building."

Pete was quiet a few moments, then said, "The Long Walk and their stay here were pure hell for the Navajos. They called it nadahadziidaa—the time we were afraid."

"You speak Navajo?"

"I know a few words. That one stuck."

We talked late into the afternoon. The baile was cranking up on the old parade ground. Someone played "La Marseillaise" on a fiddle. When it was over the singing and dancing began. I hadn't fully decided where I was headed in the morning but I was leaning toward California. It promised a clean break. Paulita couldn't come, but I could return for her once the baby was born and the heat'd cooled. The more I thought about it the better it sounded.

"What do you think, Kid?" I finally said. "Ready to light out for California?"

"Hell yes."

"The Spanish Trail runs from Santa Fe to Los Angeles. Folks don't use it much anymore, but I reckon we won't get too lost long as we keep going west. Could look at the Chama country along the way. Do a little prospecting for Navajo gold. Sound good to you?"

"You bet."

That pretty much settled it.

CHAPTER 11 **Antrim**

Garrett was pretty well shook up, as he didn't want it said that he had killed the wrong man.

—PETE MAXWELL, AS TOLD TO BUNDY AVANTS, DATE UNKNOWN

AFTER A WHILE THE FIDDLE stopped and harp music kicked in. I'd never heard a harp. It was sad. Beautiful. Not what you'd expect at a baile. I looked at Pete.

"Turlough O'Carolan," he said. "A blind Irish harpist. I met him on the plaza in Santa Fe playing for pesos. Invited him over. He rode in on a horse. By himself. Pretty good trick for a blind man."

Pete got up to leave.

"Better check on the party. I'll send Paulita after dark."

Jesus Silva showed up a little later. He knew both me and Pat were in town. He figured his house was safer than Celsa's. Kid and me talked it over and decided he was right.

When Celsa came into the kitchen I told her we were leaving.

"Tell Paulita," I said.

"Ser prudente."

We slipped out the back and went to Jesus' choza three doors away. We left our horses in Celsa's corral. Later that night Kid said he was hungry.

"I got frijoles," Jesus said.

"Ain't you got carne?" Kid said. "I been eating frijoles and tortillas near a week."

"Only frijoles. Señor Pete has carne on his pórtico. Que no le importará."

"Will you cook it?"

"A bad idea," I said. "Someone could recognize you."

"I ain't Mex. Can't live on frijoles and tortillas ever day."

"Aqui," Jesus said as he handed Kid a knife. "You get Señor Pete's carne and I will cook it."

Kid took the knife and a candle and went out. The only sound from the parade ground was a mournful tune from the harp. Jesus lit a fire in the woodstove. I leaned back in my chair against the wall. Kid hadn't been gone but a few minutes when I heard a gunshot. I jerked upright and nearly fell out of the chair. Grabbed my Colt and ran out. The gunfire came from Pete's direction. The moon was high. I could see pretty good. I went through the gate into Pete's backyard. Someone was in the shadows beside the house. A side of beef was hanging on a porch beam. Kid's candle was on the rail a few feet away. Kid was lying on the porch. I felt a sharp pain in my jaw. A bullet struck me in the cheek and knocked out a couple of teeth. Another bullet hit me in the shoulder. I turned and ran behind a row of casas, throwing lead over my shoulder. Blood was running down my throat, gagging me.

Another bullet creased my head like a hot poker. I fell forward into the dirt. Couldn't think straight but figured if I laid there I'd be dead for sure. My mouth was clogged with blood. I spit out a tooth and stumbled past more casas. Could hardly see where I was going for the blood in my eyes. All I could think was, run.

The music'd stopped. Folks on the parade ground were yelling. Lights appeared in windows. A door opened. Jesus' sister grabbed my arm and pulled me in. I fell into her kitchen and passed out. When I came to I was on the floor. Jesus' sister was putting beef tallow on my head to stop the bleeding. She'd seared my shoulder and wrapped it with a rag. Celsa was there too.

"Can you hear, Bilito? Can you hear?"

My head was reeling and I wasn't for sure who was calling me. It took a bit before the words made sense. Celsa said Pat was holed up in Pete's house, afraid to come out or let anyone in. He knew it was Kid he'd killed. Jesus was building a coffin. Others were digging a grave. Pat wanted Kid in the ground before daylight.

"I'm kinda shot up, Celsa. How bad?"

"You okay. Bullets go through. I think they hit nothing bad. Nothing is broken."

Her words were encouraging but Celsa was crying.

"I busted some teeth."

"I think your teeth bleed the most. Holes they heal. Frank Lobato will take you to his sheep camp. You stay till you can ride. Then you go far away. Away from New Mexico. Go. Go. If Patricio finds you he will kill you for sure. Don't come back. La muerte awaits you here."

A few minutes later Frank was at the door.

"Tengo su caballo," he whispered into the house.

"Ayuda a Bilito a subirse a su caballo," Celsa said.

Frank came into the kitchen. He stood at my head and slipped his hands under my shoulders, then he sat me up on the floor. I near passed out from the pain. He slid his hands around my chest and clasped them together, then he pulled me straight up from the back. It was all I could do to keep my legs rigid and the vomit inside. Celsa reached around my waist. Frank and her walked me out to Buck and hoisted me up. Ain't sure I ever hurt more.

"My six-shooter. Where's my six-shooter?"

Celsa's sister was in the doorway. She went in and brought out my Colt.

"Gracias. Celsa, gracias. Por favor, tell Paulita lo siento, la amo."

Frank and me rode out of town. We kept to the shadows past half a dozen casas till we got to the parade grounds. The gunfire had brought the baile to an end. Only the harpist was still around. He was playing "Brian Boru," an old tune Aunt Cat used to sing about an Irish warrior who died saving his country. She sang it in Irish.

We crossed the Río Pecos and headed north toward Frank's sheep camp, keeping close to the cottonwoods. My head and shoulder felt like I'd been branded but I was alert. Trying to make sense of what'd happened. What was Pat thinking? That I was with Kid? He'd of asked around. Did he know I was there? Did Pete or Paulita say anything? Neither'd give me up. Jesus? He was building a coffin. Pat would of talked to him. Celsa? Jesus and Celsa were amigos. They'd of said nada. Who else was at Pete's house? A deputy? Celsa said someone shot at Pat's deputy. Did the deputy know me? He was a damn good shot. Or damn lucky. No, not lucky. Not in the moonlight. Was Pat coming after me? Would he come to Frank's camp?

I didn't have answers but the questions kept me in the saddle.

Frank looked after me for a week. I lay on my bedroll under a tarp in a grove of cottonwoods. Frank brought me food in the morning and evening and tended his sheep during the day. I had plenty of water and plenty of time to think. By the end of a week I was tired of my company. I was still sore but I was well enough to ride. It was time to head for California. I'd lost my compadre but I had my hide.

Paulita hung heavy in my heart but I couldn't lay around thinking about her. Her and the baby. It was driving me near crazy. Had to get my mind on other things. It was getting toward dark. A good time to travel.

"Time to head out," I told Frank when he returned at the end of the day. "You've done un buen trabajo on me. I appreciate it. Truly. I'd like to stay and work off my debt but it's too risky. Word'll get out you've been looking after me. Garrett'll come around. Me and you'll be in a stew."

"Entiendo, Billy. You malo. Wait uno, dos dias till you feel mejor."

"The quicker I get gone the better for both of us, compadre. You've been a buen amigo. Gracias. Por todo."

Frank gave me biscuits, oats, and a box of cartridges. I had some dinero. Gave half to Frank.

"Adios, amigo."

"Vaya con dios, Bilito."

As I rode off, I realized everything I owned in the world was on Buck. It didn't amount to much. But I could hunt, build a fire, defend myself. I planned to head to San Patricio. Be there in a few days. Stay with María and Manuel till I healed. They'd keep quiet. Get me whatever I needed in Lincoln. Then I'd be on my way to California. I didn't tell Frank. Safer that way. I didn't know where Garrett was and had no way of finding out. Figured to stay off the main roads. The ride gave me time to think. Thinking was all I'd done for a week but I still didn't have all the answers. Thunderstorms rumbled through my head.

Sometime in the night a storm hit. Lightning whited out the sky. It began pissing hail. My hat offered some protection but my hands stung whenever stones caught them just right. They felt like deerfly bites, then wasp stings as the thumps got harder and more frequent. Then the hail poured down in a torrent, crushing my hat. Every few minutes a stone buffaloed me. Buck and me were in trouble. I've knowed cowhands to hide under horses in a hailstorm, but I had too much regard for Buck. Besides, with lightning all around, Buck wouldn't of stood for it. Him and lightning didn't get on.

We weren't far from the old Alejandro Perea place at Stinking Springs where Charlie Bowdre'd been killed. Buck saw it the next time the night lit up and he galloped toward it. We'd almost made it when a chunk of ice walloped me so hard that I took a tumble. When I came to, the storm was over. The ground was covered in hail, some the size of hens' eggs, a few as big as my fist. The night was dark as a sack of black cats. I could barely make out the choza when the next lightning cracked. When I stumbled through the doorway Buck nuzzled me.

"Glad you found this place, old boy."

As I was uncinching the saddle I saw blood dripping through his left eye.

"Looks like you got thumped pretty good. Let's take a look."

I took a rag from my saddlebags and started to wipe away the blood. I was holding the bridle when Buck jerked his head. I fell into him.

"Easy, amigo. I won't hurt you. Your eye's okay. You caught a good one on the forehead but the devil won't take you tonight."

I balled up the rag and dabbed around the eye. Buck shook his head a couple of times but let me hold the rag against the cut. When the bleeding stopped I unsaddled Buck and unrolled my bedroll. A light rain was falling. I sat up much of the night with a smithy forging in my head. It was close to dawn when the cool humus smell of the rain put me to sleep.

CHAPTER 12 Stinking Springs

I don't want to dispute against you, Señora, but in my mind, which is the picture of my soul, I know it is not true. Maybe Pat Garrett, he give money to Billy to go to South America and write that story for the books. Maybe he kill somebody else in Billy's place. Everybody like Billy. His face went to everybody's heart.

—JOSE GARCIA Y TRUJILLO, AS TOLD TO JANET SMITH, 1936

WHEN I AWOKE THE SUN was well up in the sky. Before falling asleep I'd been thinking about the time Garrett captured me and the boys at Stinking Springs. One of the worst nights of my life. Near froze to death. Swore I'd never be back, but I'd just spent another night there, almost as bad as the first.

As I was packing the saddlebags I saw a bat on the floor in the corner of the choza.

"Buck, ole boy, we had a guest last night."

I nudged the bat with my foot, flipping it onto its belly.

"Got thumped like us. Made it here, then went to its maker."

I picked it up by the scruff and held it up for inspection. It was no bigger than a field mouse. The face was black and ugly as the bung hole of a mule and the body was covered with brown fur, but it was the wings that caught my attention. Folded tight against the body. Like leather. I'd never seen a bat up close. I pulled the tip of a wing out to its full length. The bat opened its eyes. I was startled and dropped its scruff but held onto the wing. It flapped its free wing and swung face first into my wrist. I let go and the bat fell to the ground. I'd felt a pinprick and wondered if it'd nailed me. No marks on my wrist. I nudged the bat again with my boot. It showed no further interest in life.

"Okay, Buck, let's leave Señor Bat alone. Maybe he'll make it. Maybe he won't."

I put the rest of my gear in the saddlebags, then I led Buck out of the choza and climbed into the saddle. It was a beautiful cloudless July morning. Planned to stay off the roads, head into the mountains, lay up till dark.

Four days later, traveling at night with the aid of moonlight and sleeping off the road during the day, I arrived in San Patricio. As I rode up to the Montoya casa María rushed out. She was crying.

"Bilito! I hear you dead!"

I slid off Buck and wrapped her in my arms.

"Wasn't me, María. It was Kid Antrim. Garrett's deputy shot me up pretty good. But I ain't a spook."

"What happened, Bilito? What happened? Your face! Your beautiful face!"

"Ain't as bad as it looks. Lost a couple of teeth is all. Won't be kissing pretty girls for a while. None like you anyway," I said as I kissed her. "Is Manuel here?"

"He is working with his tío today," she said. "He will be back para la cena."

"Think you could put me and Buck up for a day or two?"

"Of course, Bilito. Take care of your horse, then come inside."

I led Buck into the corral. He was visible from the road, but anyone passing would assume he was Manuel's. I went through the backdoor into the kitchen. María was tending a pot by the fire.

"Don't say nothing about me being here. I've got to skin out of the territory without folks knowing I'm alive."

"Of course, Bilito."

"Gracias, María. I ain't eaten much lately. Could you rustle up something to quiet my belly till Manuel comes home?"

"Frijoles are almost ready. Would you like a burrito? I can fry huevos."

"I'd like that. Gracias."

A few minutes later I was enjoying a fine meal with a beautiful señora across the table.

"These past few weeks have been an adventure. Reckon I'm lucky to be alive."

"God is looking after you, Bilito. He has especial plan for you."

"A special plan, huh? What is it?"

"I do not know. No one knows. You know when plan reveals itself."

"You think everybody has a special plan?"

"Si, everybody. Not everybody follows plan. Sometimes they try and fail. God gives them many chances."

"What's your plan?"

"That is only for me to know. But I will tell you this. God is in my heart. He tells me what I should do, what I should not do. He is in your heart too, talking, but you do not listen. Some day you will hear him."

I didn't have much faith in a God plan but María's words were comforting. The misery of the past weeks had near broken me. I'd left Paulita, lost Kid, almost been killed. I needed things to take a turn for the better.

CHAPTER 13 Mangel

Billy was a good boy, but he was hounded by bad men who wanted to kill him.

—PAULITA MAXWELL JARAMILLO, AS TOLD TO GOV. MIGUEL ANTONIO OTERO, DATE UNKNOWN

MANUEL RODE INTO LINCOLN A few days later and got a mess kit and a box of cartridges for me. I was feeling better. Spending time with María and Manuel had improved my mood but it was time to leave. Manuel gave me oats for Buck, and María loaded me down with dried beans, jerky, tortillas, and coffee. I could resupply in Albuquerque and I could shoot a jackrabbit or a quail. I'd have to build a fire, but the chances of running into anyone who knew me were slim.

My plan was to head west to Albuquerque, then continue north on the Camino Real. I'd pick up the Spanish Trail where it crossed the Río Grande between Santa Fe and Abiquiu then follow it to California.

Leaving Fort Sumner without Paulita near killed me. As I was leaving the Montoyas I realized I was giving up all my amigos. I shook Manuel's hand and kissed María, then I rode out.

"Vaya con dios, Bilito," María called when I was almost out of hearing.

Hasta que nos volvamos a ver, mi encantadora María, I whispered to the wind.

I wished Kid was with me. He'd of lifted my spirits. But Buck was a fine compadre and I counted on a pot-licking cur traveling with us. He'd been hanging around San Patricio for a week or two. Manuel suspected him of requisitioning one of María's chickens. Manuel was grateful when I said I'd take the thief with me. He didn't look like much. A mashed-in face like a bulldog, one ear chewed to the quick, no meat on his bones. If I fattened him up he'd be half my size. He was no Kid with a six-shooter but I figured he might prove handy. I called him Mangel on account of his ear. I spoke his name in Mexican so it'd sound like "mon-grel."

He was skittish when I first encountered him. Had a sigogglin gait. Maybe a broke leg that had healed bad. I'd tossed him biscuits and jerky to earn his attention if not his trust. When I rode out of San Patricio he followed.

The first few days on the road he held back. At times I wondered if he was still on my trail, then he'd show up at dinnertime. Every afternoon I shot small game for him. The third night Mangel slept a few feet away. The fourth night he let me touch him. When we got to Albuquerque the afternoon of the fifth day we were amigos.

It was my first time in Albuquerque. The town was smaller than Santa Fe but it felt bigger. Santa Fe was a Mexican town. Albuquerque was more American. The main street had two-story buildings made of wood with columns and cornices like you'd find back East. The plaza had adobe buildings. It'd been around since Spanish days.

I stopped at the well on the plaza and cranked the windlass. After watering Buck and Mangel I headed to the Highland Mercantile to restock. Mangel scavenged a dead rat while I went inside. When I mounted Buck again Mangel led us out of town.

Shortly we came upon a fiesta. The chords of a guitar and odors of charred meats and tamales and horse shit wafted in the breeze. Vaqueros in their charro suits and señoritas in their fanciest dresses eyed one another while caballeros and señoras eyed their daughters. It was the games that caught my attention. I joined a crowd headed to a pit surrounded by a log fence. A she bear was shackled to a post inside. Folks around the fence were chanting "Toro! Toro!" Two vaqueros rode in with a bull roped between them. His horns were wreathed in flowers. They turned the bull loose, then rode back out, shutting the gate behind them. The bull milled around the gate. The bear paced behind the post. Neither seemed anxious for an encounter. A few folks in the crowd began chanting "Sangre! Sangre!" A vaquero next to the gate slashed the bull across the nose with a knife. That got him riled. He glared at the grizzly, then lowered his head. The bear seemed almost surprised. She started to rise on her hind legs when the bull slammed into her. She tumbled backward, her jaws clamped on the bull's tongue. The bull bellowed, the crowd moaned. The bear rolled to her side but she was back up on her hind legs quick as a conejo. The bull's tongue was in tatters. So were the flowers. When the bull charged again he ripped open the bear's belly. The crowd roared its approval. The grizzly landed on her back but hung onto the bull's head. She stumbled getting back to her feet. I'd seen enough. Went back to the road and found a sport more to my liking.

A rooster was buried up to its neck. Vaqueros took turns trying to yank the bird out of the ground while racing at full speed. The rooster's head had been greased, so even if a vaquero managed to grab it he couldn't hang on. I'd seen this game at other fiestas. The object was to snatch the rooster, race to a tree a hundred paces away, and return to the start while other vaqueros tried to steal the bird from the captor.

I watched half a dozen vaqueros try their luck. Most missed the grab. One hombre fell from his saddle. Two caught the rooster but couldn't hang on. I'd learned a thing or two watching Comanches hang off the side of horses, and I had an idea about how to deal with the greasy head, but I had to act quick. The rooster's neck was cattywampus. A few more yanks and it would rip off. I lined up behind two vaqueros. The first missed completely. The next had lengthened the stirrup strap on one side. I figured he'd done this before. It looked like he'd made a good grab but he let the rooster slip through his fingers. I took a swig of water and spit on my hand, then I gigged Buck in the ribs. Three or four strides short of the target I leaned out of the saddle and dragged my wet hand through the dirt, then I grabbed the rooster's head and hung on. Buck flew past and I floated back into the saddle, the carcass flopping against my thigh, feathers flying. As we raced toward the tree, vaqueros let out whoops and started after us. We flew past the tree and kept going. Buck was fast. Several minutes later I looked behind. Not a vaquero in view. No Mangel either. I slowed Buck to a trot.

A few miles north of town Buck and me entered a grove of cottonwoods. Before long here came Mangel, his tongue hanging out. Buck and me walked toward him. He sat down on his haunches then fell over on his side. I climbed down and petted him. Told him he was a good boy. After a bit he stood up and went down to the river to get a drink, then he commenced trotting up the road. Buck and me fell in behind.

A couple of miles on, Mangel stopped to sniff something beside the road. I couldn't see it but I heard the rattle. Mangel reared backward. The snake struck. Mangel yelped. I gigged Buck and drew my six-shooter. Buck jumped forward and I fired twice as the snake pulled back to strike again. It fell into its coils. Mangel limped off on three legs. I leapt off Buck and started to pick up the snake and sling it into the brush, but then I remembered an ole boy who got bit by a rattler after cutting off its head. He had seizures and lost his sight. Near died. I left this one where it lay.

When I approached Mangel he limped away.

"Come on, amigo. Let me help you."

I didn't know what I could do for him but I knew he shouldn't be walking around. If I'd start toward him he'd start away.

"Well, Mangel, I'm gonna set up camp. Join me when you can."

I led Buck into the cottonwoods and unsaddled him. Laid out my bedroll and supplies and built the first fire since San Patricio. I'd been soaking frijoles in a pouch in my saddlebag. I dumped them in a pot of fresh water from the river and set it on the fire to simmer. I cleaned the rooster and put it in a skillet to cook. Mangel caught the scent and hobbled over. He lay down on the opposite side of the fire. I stood up and started toward him. He stumbled trying to get up. I sat back down.

"Okay, boy. I'll leave you alone."

I poked at the bird with my knife. Mangel lay back down and took a few licks at his front paw. He was drooling, in serious pain. When the bird was cooked I ripped off a leg and held it out for Mangel. His nose began twitching. He raised up on his good legs and hobbled toward me. I leaned forward. He snatched the leg and devoured it, bones and all. A minute or two later he puked it up. I ate my beans and the second leg, then cleaned my mess kit, staying away from Mangel the whole time.

I kept the fire going well after dark. A comfort to me if not to Mangel. I slept fitfully and awoke several times during the night. The moon was up. Mangel lay near the fire ring, twitching like a leaf in the wind. I feared that if I went toward him he might wander off. Didn't want him to die in the brush. When I awoke at first light he hadn't moved. His front paw was swollen double. He looked up at me without lifting his head. He was panting and whimpering. I started to touch his paw but he pulled it back.

We stayed in the cottonwoods near a week. We were tucked out of sight from the road and saw only a few hombres. Mangel slept most of the time. I made one trip to Albuquerque. Wasn't sure if Mangel would stick around while I was gone, but when I returned he hadn't moved. The swelling had gone down and he let me touch his paw. The next day he was moving around almost like his old self.

"Looking good, old boy. What do you say we head up the road?" I climbed into the saddle. Mangel wagged his tail and trotted back toward the road. It was good to be moving again.

We didn't make much progress the next couple of days. Mangel didn't have his usual granite, and he rarely left the road, but he walked a solid pace. That suited me. I'd had a fearsome headache for a couple of days and couldn't shake it.

Late in the afternoon of the third day we came across a well-traveled crossroad. I figured it might be the Spanish Trail. We followed it to the Río Grande. When we got to the ford another river was flowing in from the west. Figured it was the Chama. We crossed the Grande and headed up the Chama valley. Next day we arrived in Abiquiu.

Abiquiu's an old Tewa town. Had an army post then, but it's gone now. Indians still live there. Mainly Utes and Navajos and Apaches stolen as children by the Comanches and sold to the Spanish. Coyotes they call them.

Stopped at Gonzales's store for supplies.

"Folks ever pass this way from California?"

"Ever few months. More goin' than comin'. That'll be a dollar."

"What's the road like?"

"Pretty bad I 'spect. Easy to get lost. It's what I hear anyway."

"Any unfriendlies?"

"Jicarillas are tame. They's some Comanch up north. In the San Juans. They come down ever once in a while raisin' hell. Mean sumbitches. You don't want to run into 'em. But they ain't been around in six months. You by yourself?"

"Got me a dog and a horse."

"Your biggest threat is Ole Moze. And I do mean big. They say when he rears up he towers over a man on horseback. Unusual color too. You'll know him if you see him. He's almost yeller. He's wrecked a couple of pack trains in the past year. Killed two miners. A trapper too. Killed a soldier I knew personally."

"Thanks. I'll try to steer clear of him."

"Good luck on that. If that ole griz's got your number you won't see him comin'. A couple day's ride though and you'll be out of his territory."

I laid a coin on the counter and picked up my supplies. A few minutes later Buck and me and Mangel were headed for California.

Storm clouds were building as we headed up the Spanish Trail. The sky ahead was the color of worn gunmetal. The canyon was narrow, not more than a hundred paces across. The walls rose sheer a couple of hundred feet. The road worked its way toward the head of the canyon. It climbed out on the rim then dropped into another canyon smaller and narrower than the first. By the time we got to the second canyon the sky looked like the bore of a cannon exploding every few seconds. Thunder came in courses, growing louder and louder. Before I could untie my slicker the rain slammed into me. Rivulets of water rushed down the road ahead then pealed off the side into an arroyo twenty feet below.

A crack of lightning struck a piñon above my head. Buck reared, almost pitching me over the side. He started at a gallop. I hung on.

Mangel raced after us. Ahead was a narrow side canyon. Water was careening out of it like a herd of spooked buffalo. Buck cleared the torrent without losing stride. A second or two later Mangel cried out. I turned in the saddle but he was gone. I pulled hard on the reins. Buck ran another fifty paces before he slowed. I leapt off and peered through the rain into the canyon. Rocks were tumbling into the stream from the side canyon. I called out. The canyon roared back at me. I climbed down the rocks to the flood, scrabbled up to where the side canyon washed into the stream, then headed back downstream, calling Mangel all the time. I climbed back up to Buck. Took the reins and walked down the road looking for Mangel. Half an hour later I'd seen nothing. The cataract there was thirty feet below the road. A sheer drop.

I wrapped Buck's reins around a pine and started back up the road. The rain fell like a waterfall. When I got to where Mangel disappeared a river was pouring out of the side canyon. If the timing had been off, Buck and me could of been swept over the side too. The cataract had swelled almost to the road. If Mangel was down there I figured he was buried under a sea of water, or ripped to shreds among the rocks.

It was still raining as evening set in. Buck and me continued down the road, looking for a place to put up for the night. Just before dark we found a cavity in the cliff wall. The cliff leaned over the road, leaving enough of an overhang to keep us dry. The ground was rocky and sloped toward the flood but it was the best we'd likely find before dark. I took the saddle off Buck and rested it against the rock wall. Pulled out oats for Buck. A bowl in the rock floor a few feet away held enough water to get him through the night. I sat on my bedroll and leaned against the wall. Had no desire to eat. I sat up most of the night listening to the rain.

When I awoke in the morning, Mangel was lying beside me. He lifted his head and looked at me. I scratched him behind his chewed-up ear. He thumped his tail. He was banged up bad, covered in mud and blood. Cuts on his head and hip and front leg. When I stood up he tried the same. He made it to three legs and held up his front paw, the same one the rattler bit. I fetched a strip of jerky from my saddlebags. He wolfed it whole. I gave him another, then I sat back on my bedroll. He hobbled over and lay beside me, resting his head on my leg. I ate a strip of jerky. He ate a strip. I ate another. He ate another. We kept that up till I got to regarding my supply.

"Don't know how you made it, old boy. I'm sure glad you did. You got more lives than an old tom."

I used a rag and a pot of water to wash off the mud and blood. When I tried washing his bad leg he slid it back and began licking the wound.

"You're a ball and chain, Mangel. We lay up every few days for you to heal."

I tousled his head. He thumped his tail.

"If that's the way it is, that's the way it is."

He looked up at me. I gave him another strip of jerky.

We were on a narrow ledge where the trail climbed down the side of the canyon. The stream was forty feet below us. The canyon rose a hundred feet. A thunderstorm blew over the first afternoon but the overhang kept us dry. We stayed there another two days. I didn't sleep much. By the last morning Mangel was getting around pretty good. He was walking on all fours. Buck and me were batty as flies in a bell jar. The floodwaters had receded to a gentle run. I packed up and we headed west.

Late that afternoon I felt disoriented and light-headed. The canyon wall beside me raced past whenever I looked at it. I'd been feverish and had trouble sleeping the past few days. My head'd been busting like a pounding mill. Figured sleeping on a rock bed and fretting about Mangel was the cause. This was different. The last thing I remember was Aunt Cat blocking the trail ahead, holding up her hand like she wanted me to stop.

CHAPTER 14 **The Monastery**

I've never seen anyone that sick still hanging on to life.
Brother Jude said Billy would have had to get better before he could die.

—BROTHER CHARLES, *Diary*, SEPTEMBER 17, 1881

WHEN I AWOKE I WAS lying on a cot in a small room. A wooden cross hung on the wall at the foot of the bed. A small table and chair stood in the opposite corner. My clothes were folded on the table.

I tried to sit up but couldn't. I could slide my arms and legs sideward but I couldn't raise them. After a while I drifted back to sleep. When I awoke again an old monk in a black robe and a hood was on the chair near the foot of the bed.

"Welcome, brother. I am glad to see you alert. We worried we would lose you. You will be alright. I am Brother Jude. You are in the Monastery of St. Anselm and have been for almost a week. How do you feel?"

Brother Jude was very formal. He had a strong accent, like John Tunstall. I learned later he was the oldest of the monks. At least seventy.

I tried to talk but nothing came out.

"Your voice will come back," he said. "You have hydrophobia. A Tinde party brought you here. A di-yin has been treating you. Doctors have no cure for hydrophobia. The Tinde have a cure, but even with their medicine few survive. You are a lucky young man."

Panic sluiced through me. I'd heard about a wolf with hydro biting trappers at the last rendezvous. They acted drunk, drooled, howled, clawed theirselves, ripped off clothes. One of them was shot when he attacked his partners. The other disappeared in the Wind Rivers. I turned my head from side to side.

"Try not to move," Brother Jude said. "The worst is over. Your faculties will return. For now you need rest."

When I awoke again Brother Jude was entering the room with a bowl of broth.

"Good. How do you feel today?"

"Buck . . . Mangel." I slurred the words.

"Your horse and dog? They are fine. When the Tinde brought you here they brought your horse. The dog followed. He was in bad shape. Like he had been in a terrible fight, but he is resting and eating now. His wounds are healing. We have another dog here. Scout. They have become friends. Next time I will bring your dog. For now let us see if you can eat."

Brother Jude sat beside the bed and spooned broth into my mouth. I had trouble swallowing. I coughed and sputtered. The old monk waited between spoonfuls, wiping my mouth after each draft. After the soup reached my belly I began to feel better.

Brother Jude was good to his word. When he opened the door on his next visit Mangel bounded in and leapt onto the bed. He flopped down beside me and laid his chin on my face. His head was almost as big as mine. I could barely breathe but I began laughing.

Brother Jude talked for the next hour, mostly about the Jicarillas who lived nearby. He called them Tinde. Said they helped build the monastery. Said they were peaceful generous people but they were being harassed by a small band of Comanches who'd run off the reservation and were hiding in the Colorado mountains.

Over the next couple of weeks the old monk brought me grub twice a day, bathed me, and monitored my progress as my strength returned. I was sitting up by the end of the first week and standing a week later. As my voice came back we had longer talks. I told him who I was, but I left out my adventures at Fort Sumner. He could tell from my wounds that I'd been in a gunfight, but he didn't ask. I was curious about my cure.

"How did you contract the disease?" Brother Jude asked. "An animal bite?"

"I've studied on that," I said. "I've cooked lots of game, but only after I killed it. If I ate a critter with hydro could I get the disease?"

"I do not think so, Billy. The few cases I have known were caused by someone being bitten. Mostly by bats."

"Picked up a bat a while back. When it was flopping it hit my arm. Felt a prick but thought nothing of it. My wrist itched some."

"I have heard that you can be bitten by a bat and not know it."

I showed Brother Jude my arm. We didn't see no sign of a wound.

"Ain't heard of someone surviving hydro. How'd you save me?"

"We prayed, but our Tinde brothers get the credit. A di-yin named Juan Mundo arrived shortly after the Tinde brought you here. He said the time was propitious because the moon would be full in three days. I don't know what he did. He shut us out while he performed his rituals. He said it would be harmful if anyone spoke to you. When he came out of your room three days later he had painted a disk on your forehead with a dust made from galena."

"Galena?"

"It's a shiny gray mineral. It is hard to find. The Tinde have a source in the Manzano Mountains. Juan also painted your face with burnt mescal and he made a cross on your chest with hoddentin."

"Hoddentin? Never heard of that neither."

"It is a flour made from tule pollen. Juan also gave you a potion. He told us to give you some every day for a week. I suspect it was the potion that saved your life."

"What was it?"

"He did not say."

"Did you ask him?"

"He ignored my question."

"It'd sure be good to know."

"Yes it would, but I suspect you would have to be a Tinde."

"Whatever it was, I'm grateful."

"Juan made a sand painting on the floor beside your bed. A snake in the shape of a circle surrounding animals and birds. A bear, an eagle, a bat, a raven. A deer maybe. In reds, yellows, blues. And black. Juan swept it away the next day. He said it absorbed the poison from your body."

By the end of summer I was getting out near every day. I used a walking stick but I was grateful to be with Mangel and Buck. Didn't try to ride. My legs and hands pretty much ignored what I asked of them. I'd liked to of been completely well, but knowing I should of been completely dead improved my mood considerably. Besides, I liked the isolation. Figured I could hide out there indefinitely. The place was special. The canyon was half a mile wide, its walls rising hundreds of feet. The Río Chama, edged with cottonwoods and willows. It split the canyon down the middle.

I liked the company too. The monastery's where I met Carlos. He looked a little like you but he was a good bit taller. Brother Jude was a doctor. Padre Romuald was the abbot. He was the only priest. Brother Thomas was the cook. I'd worked in kitchens so I helped Brother Thomas. He didn't think much of my cooking.

I had little contact with two of the monks. A nod was about it. They were hermits. I saw them during services and in the garden when I pulled vegetables for dinner.

Then there was Brother Bede. A penitente. I'll get to him in a bit.

The only person not a monk was Raúl, a Jicarilla boy the monastery'd adopted. He had a bad leg. Horse fell with him when he was barely old enough to ride. Comanches killed his folks. There was no one else to look after him. He worked with Brother Thomas in the kitchen.

During the first few weeks, I spent time with Padre Romuald near every day. There was an aura about him. Holiness I reckon. Even when he was agitated his eyes were peaceful. He looked old, but as I think back on it he was probably about my age now. He was a Black Monk, a member of the Order of St. Benedict. So were the others. He'd been living on the Chama for near twenty years. He said that the first time he saw the Chama valley he knew it was the place he was supposed to be.

"Half a dozen of us came west in '63 from St. Vincent Abbey in Pennsylvania," he said. "After Gettysburg. The war was tearing the monastery apart. Some of us wanted to leave. Our hearts were sick over the shape of the nation. We wanted to move to the desert like St. Antony or the mountains like St. Benedict. We chose here because it had both. We thought we were getting away from the war. We were wrong, of course. Glorieta Pass ended the war in the West, but the aftermath lingered for a decade. So many lost men came of age fighting on one side or the other. Thousands of them lost their families. They had no jobs to return to. They had no skills. All they knew was killing. Hundreds came to New Mexico where there is little law to bridle them."

"I know some of them boys."

Padre smiled.

"We came here to find God. God was in Pennsylvania too, but life there was too complicated. Here we have fewer distractions."

One afternoon in early fall I told Padre about Pete Maxwell arriving at the monastery.

"I remember," he said. "We were a young community. Some of us were homesick. We were happy to see the soldiers, until they took away our friends. The Tinde were more than friends. Without their help we would not have survived. We were happy to see them return a few years later. They helped us clear the land. They helped us build our first houses. Wickiups made of sticks covered in grasses and mud and animal skins. They were cold in winter and they leaked horribly during the summer rains. Later, Mexicans from Abiquiu showed us how to make adobe bricks. How to make good solid roofs. A crew from Abiquiu came one summer and built the church. We were blessed. We still are. Life this good makes it easier to peel off the layers, see things more clearly."

"Know what you mean, Padre. But clarity comes to me when someone's shooting at me."

Over the next few weeks me and Buck and Mangel explored the canyons around the monastery. Sometimes I'd bring back a deer or jackrabbit for the brothers. During the first long cold spell Mangel jumped a mule deer and chased it onto the ice on the Chama. The deer fell through the ice and Mangel went in after it. The deer made it across but Mangel got caught in the current and swept downstream under the ice.

Me and Buck raced to where the ice broke up in some rapids. When Mangel flushed out, we waded out to get him. I grabbed him by the scruff and hung on while Buck dragged us back to the willows. Built a fire and wrapped Mangel in a blanket. He shook for an hour. I fed him some jerky. By nightfall he was back to his old self and we returned home.

I call it home because it was beginning to feel like one. There was something about the place I couldn't peg. A kind of power maybe. Monks said it was God. I wasn't so sure about that, but whatever it was I could feel it.

Cutting firewood was a major job at the monastery. As my strength returned, it became one of my tasks. One afternoon when I was returning to the monastery with a load of piñon and cottonwood kindling I met Padre Romuald coming out of the chapel. The monks sat for hours every day in the chapel. Figured it must be boring. I asked him about it.

"Is that why you're here, living in this desert like a hermit so you can work at prayer? You're practically living like an Indian."

"Do you know any Indian who would choose to live like a white man?" he said.

"Can't say as I do."

"I made no sacrifice coming here. I just simplified my life. Monks in the early Church did not go into the desert to sacrifice themselves, hoping God would bestow grace on them. They went into the desert to set aside worldly distractions. Brother Jude comes from a wealthy family. He could have had most anything he wanted, but he found wealth to be a hindrance. Sacrifice is not necessarily a good thing. It creates an expectation that God will reward us. Then the heart is no longer acting out of love. It is seeking a reward. Grace is not a reward. It is a gift. It comes to us unbidden, regardless of who we are or what we've done."

I wasn't sure I understood Padre so I asked a simpler question.

"Why does God want us to pray? If God is God why does he need our prayers?"

"Prayer does not benefit God," he said. "Prayer helps us become kinder, more compassionate, more loving."

"Kindness and compassion sound good but they ain't worth a peso in these parts. They're a hindrance to survival."

"In a sense you are right. Kindness and compassion will not make your life easier. But they will make it better for you and those around you. And you will be happier."

"I could tolerate more happiness. I surely could, but I figure survival's my first duty. Dead men ain't much help to anybody."

Padre smiled.

"We are all trying our best to stay alive," he said.

CHAPTER 15 Brother Charles

We travel only as far as we can, never as far as we want.

—BROTHER CHARLES, *Diary*, AUGUST 4, 1881

ONE FALL MORNING AFTER BREAKFAST I walked back to the cloister with Carlos. I called him Brother Charles because that's what the monks called him. The sky to the east was on fire. The temperature had dropped in the night and it'd snowed. Barely enough to cover the ground. The piñons and junipers stood out against the white slopes across the way. Magpies called from the willows along the Chama.

Brother Charles asked if I'd like a cup of tea. Coffee was my drink of choice and still is. More than this rotgut we're drinking. But I was growing partial to tea. Especially the Ceylon tea Brother Charles kept in his room. The storekeep at Gonzales's in Abiquiu would get him more when he ran out.

We passed through the gate into the cloister. When we got to Brother Charles' cell he chunked a couple of logs in the stove and set on a kettle to boil.

"I picked up extra biscuits at breakfast," he said. "Would you like one?"

"I would. Thanks. I make a decent biscuit but Brother Thomas's are better."

"I wouldn't have pegged you for a baker."

"I ain't bad."

"I'm sure you aren't. When you're feeling stronger would you like to work with Brother Thomas and Raúl in the kitchen?"

"Be happy to."

There was something about Brother Charles that was different from anyone I'd ever met. I trusted him immediately. He was younger than most of the monks. More worldly. He was interested in things I was interested in. Nature, history, Indians. I could talk to him about anything. Aside from Padre Romuald he was the most honest hombre I've ever met.

While we were drinking tea I told him about my life. The troubles in Lincoln, my plans for California. I told him about Kid and about the time he nearly died. Would have if it hadn't of been for a nun. Sister Blandina.

"She was a saint," I said.

"Really?"

"I figured she was. She looked like one."

"I didn't know saints have a look."

"They all have halos."

"Sister Blandina had a halo?"

"She did. Kid Antrim got shot in Trinidad, Colorado. He was in bad shape. Doctors knew who he was. They wouldn't touch him. Not Sister Blandina. She fixed him up proper. I went to Trinidad to bring him home. When I saw him, there she was, glowing like a torch. I don't mean a little halo like in pictures. She lit up the room. Figured she had to be a saint. She worked a miracle on Kid. He should of been dead."

"You have a fine mind, Billy," Brother Charles said as we were finishing our tea. "You know a lot for a lad your age. Where did you get your education?"

"Made it to the fourth grade. Got most of my learning from books."

"The fourth? That's as far as you got?"

"Yeah. It's kind of a funny story. A couple of boys behind me in class were cutting up. The teacher, Miss Belmont, whacked them across the head with a ruler. I snickered. She whacked me across the back of the hand. I mean to tell you it hurt. When she turned around I came out of my chair and cracked her over the head with a geography book. Knocked her flat on her butt. I ran out the door. Never went back."

"How old were you?"

"Ten. I was a hard case."

CHAPTER 16 Brother Bede

There is always risk in being alive.
The greater the risk, the more alive you are.

—BROTHER CHARLES, *Diary*, DECEMBER 23, 1880

"EVER WORRY ABOUT RATTLERS?" I asked.

Brother Charles and me were taking our daily walk after breakfast. Brother Charles was wearing sandals. It'd been freezing during the night but the sun was out and the air was beginning to warm.

"Not at this hour," he said. "A few are still around. Most of the locals have left for a den down the river a ways."

"I've heard of snake dens. Never seen one."

"It's an impressive sight. Hundreds of them come from all over. They lay out in the sun before holing up for the winter. Would you like to see it?"

"I would."

"Brother Bede's asked about it. I'll check with him. See if we can go this afternoon. Maybe we can catch them before they go underground."

We were hiking a trail leading out of the canyon. Mangel and Scout were with us. We stopped to catch our breaths. I tickled Mangel behind the ears. His tongue was hanging out.

"Suppose you got snakebit," I said. "What would you do? No horses. You couldn't ride for help."

"Brother Jude'd pump me up with whiskey, then he'd suck out the poison and inject the bite with ammonia. But I'd put more trust in Juan Mundo. He's the di-yin who treated your hydrophobia. When Brother Thomas was bit, Juan treated him with herbs and wrapped his ankle in a tobacco poultice. The Tinde have remedies that go back centuries. Sometimes they work. Brother Thomas was lucky. But if a rattler hasn't eaten for a month and he gets a taste of you? You'd better have a strong constitution and the grace of God."

"Mangel got bit back in the summer. He was sick a few days. You think he had God's grace?"

"Maybe. I don't think dogs are as sensitive to snakebite as we are. My father hunted coyotes and wolves. Sold the hides. Almost every hide I saw—and I saw hundreds—was riddled with snakebites. I doubt there'd be a coyote or wolf around if snakes killed them as easily as they kill us. Probably true for dogs too."

Long about midafternoon Brother Charles and me left with Brother Bede to see the snake den. The day'd warmed up enough Brother Charles figured the snakes'd be out sunning theirselves.

I haven't told you about Brother Bede. He often went with us on walks. I liked him. He was from Sonora. After his ma died of cholera during the Apache War, him and his pa and his brothers headed for California. He was six. Apaches attacked the wagon train on the Jornada del Muerto. His pa was killed. The brothers got split up among different families. He ended up in Magdalena, living on a farm with a penitente hermano and his family. He joined the Brotherhood when he was fifteen. A year later he left Magdalena. Planned to walk to California. A couple of weeks out he stopped at St. Anselm's for the night. Stayed a week, then stayed for good. He became a monk but he remained a penitente. Him and Brother Charles were amigos. I think Brother Charles knowed his family. He mentions them in his diary.

Before leaving we'd put up Mangel and Scout. We followed a trail downstream along the Chama a couple of miles then turned back east up a side canyon.

"A couple of weeks ago we'd have seen tarantulas on the march," Brother Charles said. "They come down this canyon every year."

"I've seen them on the move in Texas," I said. "Often wondered where they were headed."

"The males are the travelers. Females stay put and wait for males to show up. The ladies eat their lovers after mating is over."

"I'm glad they are not marching now," Brother Bebe said. "I'd druther step on a rattlesnake."

"They aren't poisonous," Brother Charles said. "The bite's like a bee sting."

"They are big and ugly. That is enough for me."

Ten minutes later we came to a gravely outcrop. A dozen feet below were hundreds of rattlers tangled together like piles of rope. Rope alive and smelling of burnt sugar.

"The dens are under the rocks," Brother Charles said. "The snakes come out on warm afternoons. Soon they'll den up for the winter. When spring arrives they'll head home."

Brother Bede kicked a stone. It clattered down the rock and dropped among the snakes. Some scattered into burrows, some into the grass. The dry rattling hum of their tails grew louder and louder.

"Devils in the pit of hell," Brother Bede said. "I see why Satan in the Garden was a snake. Forget what I said about rattlesnakes. I'm not getting close to those vipers."

"You reckon Satan was a viper?" I said.

"Can we go now?" Brother Bede said.

About then a tarantula crawled up over the edge of the ledge.

"Look here," Brother Charles said. "You've stirred up a late lover, Brother Bede."

"Where!"

Brother Bede spun around to face the spider. He slipped on the gravel as he turned, falling backward over the edge. His screaming stopped when he hit the ground. Dozens of rattlers struck as they slithered over him. His arms disappeared, then his chest. His face and legs, still jerking, floated above a sea of writhing bodies. Terror fixed in his eyes. Then he sank beneath the swell.

"Oh God!" Brother Charles cried as he started to climb down the rocks.

I grabbed him and pulled him back.

"You can't help."

"I can't leave him."

"You ain't got a choice."

He tried to pull away.

"You go down there, I'll have two bodies to bring home."

He sat on the ledge and wept.

While Brother Charles sat in silent prayer I gathered branches and vines to make a travois. By late afternoon the cold was setting in. When I looked over the ledge the snakes were gone. Brother Bede lay on his back, his clothes torn, his face a morass of caked blood. We climbed down and laid him on the travois. His eyes were milking over. Brother Charles closed them. As we were leaving I shot a couple of stragglers heading to the den.

It was near dark when we got back to the monastery. Padre Romuald met us at the cloister gate, his eyes tearing.

"I feared trouble when you missed vespers," he said.

When the bell rang for vigils next morning I was already awake. Got dressed and went to the chapel. It was bitter cold. The moon had set. The sun wouldn't be up for a couple of hours. Stars lit up the canyon. Coyotes yapped at one another across the way.

Most of the monks were in their stalls. I took a bench in the back and listened as the monks chanted the psalms. Brother Bede was dressed in his monk's robe, lying on a cooling board before the altar. He was unrecognizable. During Mass Padre Romuald talked about Brother Bede, who he was, where he came from. That's when I learned most of what I told you about him.

After Mass the monks carried him to a rise overlooking the Chama and laid him in the ground. Raúl had dug the grave during the night. The sky was beginning to lighten. Stars were fading. Magpies were jabbering down by the river. Padre Romuald said a few prayers. The monks chanted psalms again. When they finished, each of them dropped a shovelful of dirt into the grave. Padre stuck a cross of fir into the ground next to Brother Bede's head. Then the monks walked in twos back to the cloister, chanting. Raúl filled in the grave. I offered to help but he said it was best if he did it alone.

CHAPTER 17 The Río Chama

All my life I have searched for something I cannot understand.

—BROTHER CHARLES, *Diary*, PALM SUNDAY MORNING, 1881

A FEW DAYS LATER BROTHER Charles and me were taking an afternoon walk along the Chama. Mangel and Scout raced ahead, nosing the thickets for rabbits. Snow from the previous week was gone. To the west, clouds were dumping a waterfall into a side canyon. If we'd been paying attention we'd of realized it was headed our way.

"The other day you said the Bible ain't factual," I said. "My Aunt Cat thought it was."

"Biblical stories aren't history although some are based on historical events," Brother Charles said. "The Garden of Eden, Noah and the flood, Jonah and the whale. Job in God's chess game with Satan. They're not supposed to be literally true. They tell us how to live our lives. The best stories are morally true. They don't have to be literally true.

"Look at the story of Jesus' Resurrection in the Gospels. Depending on which Evangelist is telling the story there are anywhere from one to five women at Jesus' tomb. They're greeted by one or two angels, or no angels at all. The tomb is open or it's closed. The women are filled with joy and tell the apostles, or they're terrified and tell no one. Most of the doctrines of Christianity rest on the facts of this story. Suppose these four versions were presented at trial in a courtroom. What would a jury make of them?"

"If the witnesses were that confused at my trial I believe I would of got off."

"I believe you would have too. The Bible is full of such discrepancies. The first chapter of Genesis says that God created plants and animals before he made man. The second chapter says that God made man, then the plants and animals. Are the contradictions important? . . . We'd better head back before we get drenched."

We'd almost made it to the monastery when the first drops hit. Brother Charles and the dogs ran ahead. I was soaked when I reached the cloister. Brother Charles was waiting on a bench on a sheltered porch. He laid a blanket over my shoulders.

As we sat there I asked him about loving your neighbor and the parable of the Good Samaritan. Aunt Cat often talked about that story. It'd always graveled my craw.

"I didn't live far from Jimmy Dolan," I said. "He was my neighbor. If I found him beat up in a ditch I'd put him out of his misery. At least out of mine. How about Comanches? They're neighbors. At times too close neighbors. What's it mean to love enemies? It's hard to love someone who wants to kill you."

"Your story about Sister Blandina a few days ago. She was a Good Samaritan. She believed in the Golden Rule. Treat others the way you'd want them to treat you."

"That's well and good but I couldn't be a Sister Blandina to the likes of Jimmy Dolan. Figure it'd get me killed."

"I understand, Billy. It's not easy. The Golden Rule shows you how to live. It doesn't show you how to love. Love comes only with practice."

CHAPTER 18 The Jemez Mountains

Answers arrive only after I stop looking for them.

—BROTHER CHARLES, *Diary*, EASTER, 1879

"WANT TO HEAD OUT TOMORROW for Cañon de los Frijoles?" Brother Charles asked one evening. "Winter could arrive most any time. This may be our best chance."

Brother Charles knew of a canyon south of the monastery that had ancient rock houses and kivas and pictures carved in the canyon walls. He figured they were made by ancestors of the Pueblo farmers living along the Río Grande.

We'd talked earlier about going but Brother Charles wanted to wait till I was strong enough. If we waited till spring I'd be in California. I thought about California near every day.

The canyon was a few days away. We'd have to do some climbing. Brother Charles figured Mangel could make it. The hardest part would be climbing out of the Chama River canyon.

Next morning after breakfast we packed enough to last a week. I figured to shoot a rabbit or two. We filled canteens with water and headed out the trail to the south. I whistled up Mangel. Scout trotted after us. Brother Charles waved him back.

"Stay," he said. "If Comanches or Old Moze come around, Padre'll want a bugler sounding the alarm."

The lower half of the canyon wall is brick red. The upper half is banded yellow in the shadows and golden in the sunlight. Ten minutes out, the trail begins to climb over boulders that fell off the cliffs after centuries of wind and rain worked them over. Beyond the boulder fields the trail is narrow and steep with sheer drop-offs.

We climbed a few hundred feet up the face of the rock. A pair of ravens flew overhead and disappeared beyond the rim hundreds of feet above us. Heights make me uneasy and I was getting uneasier with each step. I'd worked up a good sweat when the trail seemed to end. It wasn't abrupt but what stood above us wasn't a trail either. Whatever route we took would require our hands. I was beginning to question the wisdom of bringing my Winchester. Brother Charles worked his way around a ledge to the left, checking handholds on the rocks above before taking a step. If he misjudged he'd fall a hundred feet. After taking several steps he disappeared into a notch in the rock. In a moment he appeared twenty feet above me. I hadn't moved.

"You coming?" he said.

"I might of reconsidered if I'd knowed I'd be a mountain goat. This keeps up, I may have a heart attack. You do know I ain't got my balance back?"

"It's mostly scrambling after this."

"You want me to be crow meat?"

"Don't look down. Look for handholds. Don't look at Mangel."

"This rock's got my full attention."

The ledge wasn't a foot wide. Facing the wall I shuffled leftward, my toes feeling the rock beneath, my heels hanging in the ether. With my free hand I searched for crevices to put my faith in. My heartbeat jumped a notch or two. Legs felt like straw. If I were five feet off the ground I could scamper across blindfolded.

After rounding the edge of the wall I was inside a notch that angled up to Brother Charles. It wasn't a ladder but it offered solid hand and footholds. I climbed up beside Brother Charles. Mangel scrabbled up behind me, then he bounded ahead.

"One morning years ago when I was in Sonora—" Brother Charles began when we'd stopped for a break near the top of the mesa.

"You were in Sonora? When?" I interrupted.

"I grew up there."

"I was there once in the mid '70s. Did a little hunting in the Dragoon Mountains. Cochise is buried thereabouts. I dropped into Sonora to look around. I was always looking over my shoulder, figuring Cochise's spook was eyeing my scalp. I got no truck with Jicarillas and I respect Mescaleros, but the Chiricahua scare me. The only one I ever met was Mickey Free."

"Cochise was Chiricahua alright, but Mickey Free was Mexican and Irish. Of course, there may be some Indian blood mixed in with the Mexican. If not Apache, maybe Yaqui or Pima. Mickey and Cochise had a history together though. Mickey was the cause of the Apache War."

"Figured Mickey Free was Chiricahua. At least half-breed. What'd he do to earn that old Indian's enmity?"

"He was only a boy. His real name was Felix Telles. His father died when he was ten. His mother remarried. An American, John Ward. They moved to a ranch north of the Patagonias. A couple of years later an Apache raiding party stole Ward's stock and kidnapped Felix. Ward was angry. Not over Felix. Over his stock. He asked the army for help. Lieutenant George Bascom was assigned the task.

"Bascom assumed the Chiricahua were responsible. He arranged to meet with Cochise at Apache Pass. Cochise showed up with his family. He told Bascom that it was the White Mountain Apaches, not the Chiricahua, who raided the Ward ranch. He offered to help get Felix back. Bascom called Cochise a liar and tried to arrest him. Cochise escaped but his family was captured.

"The Butterfield Stage had a way station at the Pass. Cochise captured the stationmaster and some passengers to trade for his family. Bascom said he wouldn't trade without Felix and the stock.

"Cochise was a man of integrity. It was stupid for Bascom not to negotiate. Both sides paid a heavy price. Cochise butchered his hostages and Bascom hanged his. Cochise's family hung from the trees till the ravens cut them loose. That started the Apache War. Cochise fought the army for a decade. He finally quit before he died. Cancer I think. Bascom was already dead. Killed in the Battle of Valverde. Cochise signed a treaty and moved to the Chiricahua Reservation. Of course that didn't end the war. Gerónimo's kept it alive ever since.

"A decade later Felix showed up as a military scout working with Tom Horn. His Apache name was too hard to pronounce. Tom Horn called him Mickey Free after a character in a novel. The name stuck. He's built a reputation for himself. He speaks English, Spanish, every dialect of Apache. Some Comanche too. Even a little Kiowa. I've heard he's the best scout in the army. Gerónimo hates him. Blames him for his troubles. If Gerónimo's ever captured I expect Felix will have a hand in it."

"How come you to know so much about him?"

"He's my brother."

It was a magnificent morning when we reached the crest of the mesa. The air was crisp, the sky cloudless. Far below, the cottonwoods traced the path of the Río Chama across the canyon floor.

"Believe we've been blessed this morning, Brother Charles."

"Blessed indeed, Brother Billy. What could go wrong on a day like this."

As we continued up the mountain, the piñons and junipers gave way to ponderosas. Huge trees, tall and straight, bare of branches the first fifty feet. The ground was buried a foot thick in pine needles. The calls of nuthatches and jays echoed through the forest. The trees put out an incense that smells like vanilla. I've heard of forests being a kind of cathedral. This was that kind of place.

"When we got off on Mickey Free I was telling you about an adventure in Sonora," Brother Charles said. "I was walking in the mountains one morning. Not much younger than you. I saw a rattlesnake curled up under a rock ledge. A rock squirrel happened by and stopped right in front of the snake. With his front paws he kicked dirt onto the snake. You'd think that after catching a face-full of dirt the snake would strike at the squirrel. It just lay there. Before long it was completely covered. The squirrel seemed satisfied and sauntered on. In a few minutes a towhee hopped by. When it was within range the snake exploded from under the ledge and grabbed it. When the bird stopped flopping, the snake swallowed it, head first, then disappeared under the rock."

"What was the squirrel doing?"

"I don't know."

Later in the morning we were climbing up a rocky ledge. Brother Charles was behind me. Off to my right I heard a rattle not more than a foot or two from my head. I reached for my six-shooter and fired about the time the rattler launched off the ledge. His head exploded just before he slammed into my chest.

"¡Puta madre! That ole boy scared the piss out of me. My nerves ain't as steady around rattlers as they are around Dolan's boys."

That's the second time I've had a run-in with a striking snake. The first time was in a saloon in Mora. Fred Waite was with me. The saloon keeper kept a rattler in a glass jar on the bar. I told your brother about it.

"You touch that jar," Fred said, "that snake'll strike. You'll jump like a jackrabbit."

"I wouldn't," I said.

"You wouldn't huh?"

"No, I wouldn't."

"You'd be the first. A blind man couldn't hang on when that there rattler strikes."

"Then I'm the first."

"You seem pretty sure of yourself," the barkeep said.

"Yessir."

"I'll tell you what. I'll bet you a double eagle to a quarter eagle you can't hold your finger against that jar for thirty seconds."

Fred tried to talk me down but I wasn't about to pass on the bet.

"This'll be the easiest money I ever earn," I said.

The barkeep laid a double eagle on the bar.

"Show me your money, son."

I fished a coin out of my pocket and slapped it on top of his. I reached over and touched the jar.

"Start counting."

When the snake struck I near fell off the stool. After the second try, the barkeep gave me a whiskey to steady my nerve. I was a double eagle poorer when I left and would of lost my six-shooter if Fred hadn't of dragged me out.

That night Brother Charles and me camped among the ponderosas on the side of the Jemez Mountains. It was a crisp fall evening. The moon was out. The pine needles were soft. A lion'd left his scrape a little down the hill. A day-old pile of pine straw big as a man's head, reeking of cat piss. Mangel studied it while I fixed supper. A porcupine ambled by to inspect the new neighbors.

"This day's as good as it gets," I said over supper. "I'm as content as a cat in a hamper."

"I know what you mean, Billy. Today was close to a mystical experience for me."

"Ain't sure what you mean."

"Mystical?"

"Yeah."

"It's a tough concept. *Mystical* means . . . well, coming directly from God. Padre Romuald's a mystic. His mind is not clouded by the anger, the fear, the turmoil that race through our minds, always looking for answers. Mystics just are. They accept things as they are. The rest of us are looking instead of seeing. Listening instead of hearing. I suspect that animals aren't looking for answers. They just are. Wanting answers makes us human. Did the rock squirrel want answers? We do. That's why you asked me what the squirrel was doing. How about the rattlesnake? Or the rattlesnake in the jar? Does Mangel? Mangel just is. He may have a better grip on reality than us more rational beasts."

After Brother Charles was snoring I lay in my bedroll pondering what he meant when he said Mangel just is. A porcupine nosed around the campsite. Porcupines like the salt on outhouses. Maybe this one was after the salt on the jerky. He for sure wasn't after answers. I chunked a pinecone at him. He ran into the outer dark. I drifted off to sleep.

Next morning Brother Charles kicked my bedroll. He set a cup of coffee and a couple of biscuits beside my head. When I crawled out Mangel was nowhere in sight.

“Something caught his interest,” Brother Charles said. “A wapiti passed through before daylight. Maybe that’s it. If he’s not back when we leave, he’ll find us soon enough.”

Mangel showed up when I was finishing my coffee. He slinked into camp and crawled under my knees. Hackles were up.

“What’s the matter, boy? Something bothering you?”

“We’d best pack up and move out,” Brother Charles said. “If Mangel didn’t like what he saw, we probably won’t either.”

The woods were deadly quiet. That time of morning we should of heard jays, ravens, nuthatches, something. I strapped on my six-shooter and picked up my Winchester.

A few minutes later we were headed south toward Frijoles Canyon. We didn’t know what had spooked Mangel so we walked in silence till the sun was well up in the sky. Mangel stuck close to my side.

We came to the edge of a mesa overlooking the Río Grande valley. Off to the east the Sangre de Cristos were white from the first snow. A cool wind rose up from the valley a thousand feet below. The cottonwoods lining the river were a ribbon of gold. A pair of hawks floated below the lip of the mesa.

“Cottonwoods are glorious this time of year,” Brother Charles said. “Wonder if Coronado saw them when he passed this way, what, three, four hundred years ago? Searching for something he never found. The real gold was right here. How many centuries have cottonwoods been changing colors? Thousands? Hundreds of thousands? How many centuries have we marveled at them? Maybe the hawks have seen them all.”

CHAPTER 19 Cañon de los Frijoles

The rock is so soft that in many places it can be scooped out or detached with the most primitive tools, or even with the fingers alone.

—ADOLPH BANDELIER, *The Delight Makers*

WE SPENT THE SECOND NIGHT in a high mountain valley. Cañon de los Frijoles was a couple of hours ahead. When we awoke at first light wapiti were grazing nearby. I shot a bull and smoked strips from its rump.

The trail led out of the valley and across a mesa, passing around the upper ends of several canyons. The walking was easy. The ground was soft from a light snow that had fallen during the night. The snow was mostly gone by mid-morning. Mangel was the first to see the tracks.

"Bad news," Brother Charles said.

"Bear news," I said.

"Old Moze," Brother Charles said. "His right front foot gives him away. He was here this morning."

We stopped to listen. The air was calm and clear. A flock of jays called from across the way.

"The storekeep at Gonzales's said Moze is hard on trappers," I said.

"He probably lost his toes to a trap," Brother Charles said. "But he doesn't pick only on trappers. Many a traveler hasn't made it home when Moze is about. He's legendary among the Tinde. Practically a god."

Mangel sniffed the tracks. He wasn't a barker but he'd growl if danger was near. He was growling and his hackles were up. A flock of ravens flew into a ponderosa forty feet in front of us. They croaked for a moment then flew back down the trail.

"Could be Moze," Brother Charles said. "The ravens may be asking us to follow them, hoping we'll kill him and leave them the spoils."

"If these ravens ain't lying we shouldn't crowd him."

We left the trail and went to an opening where we could watch for an ambush. Brother Charles picked up a pinch of pine dust and dropped it. It fell to his feet.

"At least we're not upwind," he said.

We stayed in the opening a good while. The ravens didn't return. When the sun was high overhead and Moze hadn't wandered our way, we went back to the trail and headed toward the canyon. The day'd warmed considerably. The sun felt good. Mangel followed a trail a short distance before coming back to us. His hackles'd settled. A couple of hours later we arrived at the head of the Cañon de los Frijoles.

"The Cochiti were the last Pueblo people here," Brother Charles said. "This is the escape route they took when the Spaniards tried to roust them off the mesa."

"What got into the Spaniards' craws?"

"They wanted the Cochiti to live in the valley near the Camino Real. Build churches. Become good Catholics."

"You think it was a bad idea?"

"It was a bad idea. I liked them being heathens. They're good honest people living with the land, not ripping it apart. Besides, the Spaniards killed them, or worse, cut off their hands and feet. We haven't improved them by making them Catholic either."

"Is that Benedictine doctrine?"

"No, but Benedictines don't believe the Church is the only route to salvation. And we don't believe in killing over religion. Or for any other reason."

The path into the canyon was little more than a game trail, hardly a trail at all. When we reached the canyon floor a flock of cranes flew over the ridge, croaking. They cut across the canyon in single file and disappeared over the wall on the opposite side. Their wingspans were wide as a man's outstretched arms.

"Headed home," Brother Charles said.

When we reached the Río de los Frijoles we followed it downstream. We'd gone a short distance when we met half a dozen Cochiti Indians with a white man. Adolph Bandelier from Illinois. The Cochiti brought him to see the rock houses their ancestors built.

One of the Indians had a broke leg and was washing it in the creek. He'd been climbing the cliff to reach a rock house when he fell. Bone was sticking out of his shin. Brother Charles stepped in. He was no Brother Jude but his gentle ways convinced the Cochiti he knew what to do.

I spent the next day with Bandelier and the Indians. We climbed among the rock houses while Brother Charles cared for his patient. Bandelier said the rock was volcanic and soft enough that Indians could cut it with stone tools. One of our companions talked about his ancestors living there hundreds of years earlier. He said they built houses against the canyon wall. They carved rooms into the wall from the upper floors of the houses. Mainly for storage and sleeping. When the houses were abandoned and fell into rubble, the rooms were exposed like caves high up in the wall.

I asked about the birds and animals that had been carved into the canyon wall dozens of feet above the ground. The Indians wouldn't talk about them. Brother Charles said they were religious pictures. No Indians would talk about them.

Next morning Brother Charles and me said goodbye to our compadres and started back toward the monastery.

The first night out we set up camp in a meadow high in the mountains. I walked down the ridge into the ponderosas looking for firewood. On the way back I found a dead raven in the duff. Picked it up. Thought I'd make a hatband from its skin. A raven croaked in the trees overhead. In a few minutes there were several more. Dozens were squawking by the time I got back to camp.

"Seems you've caused a ruckus," Brother Charles said.

"Wasn't what I expected."

"Do you remember where you found it?"

"I do."

"You should probably put it back."

The ravens kept up a commotion as I carried the dead bird back to the ponderosas. When I laid it on the ground they stopped squawking.

"You think that ole boy was king of the cuervos?" I said when I got back to camp.

"I don't know. Apparently we're not the only birds who honor our dead."

I had another dream about Aunt Cat that night. She'd led me to a rock outcrop overlooking a small lake in the wedge of a valley between two mountains. The lake was formed by a landslide across a river. Dead trees were standing in the water like stalks of grass in a wet-weather pond. Most of the branches were gone. The few that were left were raven roosts. Dozens of ravens in the trees were facing the late-afternoon sun. Aunt Cat was looking down at the birds. When I looked at her she looked at me. Then I woke up.

Next morning I told Brother Charles about the dream. I said that whenever Aunt Cat shows up with a raven or two in my sleep someone close to me dies. Sometimes within a day or two.

"Have you ever watched Mangel dream?" Brother Charles said.

"I have. He can be lying on his side, eyes slitted, only the whites showing. His legs'll kick like he's on a tear. Chasing a bear. Or a bear's chasing him. Once, he sprang up and knocked over my coffee pot without waking."

"Dogs see things in their sleep," Brother Charles said, "and they probably understand them. Why else would they dream? If dreams help dogs understand the world, surely they can help us too. I think dreams are like paintings we send to ourselves. They're full of signs and symbols. Apaches consider ravens a symbol of death. Apparently they mean the same to you. Your aunt is the messenger. I suppose she could appear in a dream and say, 'Billy, someone close to you will die in a day or two.' But dreams don't work like that. Maybe they're a holdover from a more primitive mind. A mind like Mangel's that doesn't have words. We rely on words to interpret dreams but words don't help much. They get in the way. Dogs don't have words. They may understand dreams better than we do.

"But, of course, that explanation doesn't explain how your dream knows what's going to happen."

CHAPTER 20 The Monks

I weep for humanity. Is there no solace in all this misery?

—BROTHER CHARLES, *Diary*, APRIL 15, 1879

LATE IN THE DAY WE arrived back to where we'd spent the first night. We made camp and crawled into our bedrolls without supper. I awoke in the night and watched the moon come up. I lay in the silence thinking about dreams. Mangel was shivering. I lifted the corner of my bedroll and he crawled in.

"What do you want to do, amigo?" I said as I pulled him next to me. "Head for California when we get back? Or wait out the winter and leave when the snow's about done? St. Anselm's been good to us. You've made a friend in Scout. Feels like home don't it."

Mangel thumped his tail against the bedroll.

We woke before daylight to the cries of jays. After a quick breakfast we were back on the trail.

Toward evening we neared the cliff overlooking the Chama. We'd avoided Ole Moze, it'd been a fine trip. The mountains across the way were catching the last rays of the sun. The snow on the peaks was a soft pink. I was gazing at the peaks when I saw the buzzards. Then I smelled the smoke.

"Mother of God," Brother Charles whispered.

He started running down the trail.

"What's happening?"

"I don't know."

Brother Charles was soon out of sight. I couldn't run because of the lingering hydro. When I reached the cliff Brother Charles was halfway down. A dozen buzzards drifted in slow circles above us. The chapel, the cloister, the stable, the outbuildings—all were smoldering in the glowing dark. There was no movement. Looked like someone lay on the ground beside the chapel but it was too dark to tell who. I didn't see anyone else. Started down the cliff trail. When I got far enough to where I had to climb, Brother Charles was running across the flat toward the chapel.

"No, no, no," his voice banked off the canyon walls.

He reached the monk and dropped to his knees. He bent over and touched his head to the monk. A wail rose up from him like the scream of a lion.

I worked my way down the cliff till I came to the ledge I'd eased around the first morning. As I started across, Mangel barked. I climbed back up and lifted him onto my shoulder. I worked my way back to the ledge, holding him and my Winchester with one arm. This time I scuttled across the ledge without a thought. Don't know how I hung onto him. When I was back on the trail I set him down. We clambered down the rest of the cliff, Mangel in the lead. When I reached the monastery Brother Charles was still on his knees, praying a psalm.

It was Padre Romuald, his face in the dirt, two arrows in his back. A third arrow through his neck had snapped when he hit the ground. He was missing a hand. He'd been scalped. It wasn't Jicarillas.

I ran past Brother Charles toward the chapel. Padre's hand and a bloody cross were lying in the dirt near the door. The massive wooden doors were still burning. The interior was a charred hulk of smoking rubble with small fires. The monks' pews and the bultos of Christ and Our Lady of Guadalupe were stacked and burning beside the altar. The roof had collapsed. The vigas were smoldering. It was too dark and dangerous to go inside. If monks were there they'd be dead. They'd hold till daylight.

I checked other buildings. Brother Charles left Padre and ran toward the cloister.

The first body I saw was Scout's, his head split open with a tomahawk. When I got to the corral I saw Raúl, the Jicarilla boy who worked in the kitchen. Tomahawked too. And scalped.

Buck wasn't in the corral. They'd took him. At least he was alive.

Another high-pitched wail rose from the back of the cloister. I ran through the smoke to reach Brother Charles. He was prostrate, his hands over his head. Beyond him were two rows of scalped heads, a stride apart, facing each other. Between them were the smoking embers of the fire that had cooked their faces. Three of the monks were buried up to their necks. Brother Jude's shoulders were partially out of the ground, his head a dozen paces away among a maze of hoofprints. It wasn't burned as badly as the others.

I hunkered beside Brother Charles. He'd risen to his knees and was reciting the rosary. His voice cracked as he said each of the sorrowful mysteries.

"Comanches," he said when he'd finished.

Probably the ones who'd jumped the reservation and were hiding in the San Juans.

I went back to Padre and picked up his shoulders. I dragged him to the other monks.

"What are you doing?" Brother Charles said.

"We can't leave them to the coyotes," I said. "Lay the padre between the monks and build a fire over them."

"We can't cremate them."

"Why not?"

"We have to bury them."

"Alright. The monks are mostly buried. We can lay Padre between them and build a mound over them."

"No. We'll give them a proper burial."

I understood. I returned to the corral and dragged Raúl back to the monks. By the time I went for Scout, night had set in. Smoldering fires provided the only light. I carried Scout back to the others. Brother Charles and me sat up the rest of the night beside our amigos. Mangel lay next to me leaning against my leg, shivering in the night air.

CHAPTER 21 **Comanches**

It is so cold that, to dig out a grave in the church,
you must first build a fire on top of the ground to thaw it.
You cannot chip it even with iron bars.

—FRAY ALONSO DE BENAVIDES,
A Harvest of Reluctant Souls: History of New Mexico

AT FIRST LIGHT I FOUND a couple of shovels near the monks. I went to the toolshed looking for a pickax. The shed was the only building that hadn't been burned. The Comanches had taken most of the tools. Only a hoe and a couple of rakes were left, hanging on the wall. I went back to the monks to get a shovel. Then I went to the rise where Brother Bede was buried and began digging graves. It was like digging through rock. I hoped the monks had a better time of it if they had to dig their own holes at the fire pit. I dug for the better part of three days, one grave for each monk. Graves for Raúl and Scout too. I figured Brother Charles might balk at burying Scout in consecrated ground. He never let on if he did.

Brother Charles dug out the bodies of the monks. They were kneeling when the dirt was heaped around them. We carried the bodies to the graveyard and laid them in the ground. Brother Charles laid Padre Romuald's hand and the bloody cross on his chest. He made crosses out of fir for each grave, then he read a psalm from his breviary. He put the breviary in Padre's severed hand. He picked up the shovel and covered the breviary and cross with dirt. He shoveled a single load on each of the other graves. When he got to Scout's grave he filled it in. Then he dropped the shovel and walked away.

It was late afternoon when I'd filled the rest of the graves and laid rocks on them to keep out varmints. I looked for Brother Charles and found him on a bench by the Chama, watching the sun settle on the mesa.

"Least they didn't burn everything," I said as I sat beside him.

Brother Charles smiled. It was the first sign of relief he'd shown.

We sat there listening to the magpies chirruping among the cottonwoods. A pair of ravens played high overhead. One of them carried a seedpod to the top of the canyon wall then dropped it. The second raven dove down and caught it before it hit the ground. They repeated the game with the roles reversed.

"They probably learned that game from us," Brother Charles said. "Brother Thomas and I used to throw balls to each other out here."

The yellows and reds on the canyon wall across the valley grew deeper and richer as the shadows darkened.

"I'll miss this place," Brother Charles said.

Then he turned to me.

"Are you hungry?" he said.

"Pickings are slim, Brother Charles. I could jump up a jackrabbit."

"Carlos," he said.

"Carlos?"

"Carlos. The monastery's gone. The monks are gone. Brother Charles died with them. At least he should have. Carlos is all that's left. If you can find a jackrabbit I'll get a fire going."

A wall of clouds was creeping down the canyon from the north. The temperature began to drop.

"What're you planning?" I asked.

"Tomorrow I'll go to the Tinde village. Tell them what happened. Tell them about Raúl. After that? I don't know. I'll come back for a few days. Sort things out. The brothers have been here twenty years. They deserve a fitting memorial service. The Navajo mourn for four days. They have a beautiful prayer that comforts me whenever I'm losing my moorings.

'With beauty before me I walk. With beauty behind me I walk. With beauty around me I walk.' It ends with, 'It is finished in beauty.' I don't see my life here ending in beauty. I'm left without brothers, books, vocation. God? All destroyed. This is dangerous country. We knew it. Padre often reminded us of Jesus' passive resistance. What did it get him? Torture and death. The brothers too. They were good men. Padre was a saint. So was Brother Jude. Martyrs. Maybe I wasn't fit to be with them. To die with them."

"Maybe God ain't ready for you," I said.

"I don't know, Billy. I'm bereft. If God wants more of me he'll have to show me a path. St. John of the Cross talked about a dark night of the soul. I thought I knew what he meant. I see it now. The night's so black I've lost sight of my soul. You asked me once why I came to the monastery. I said I was seeking God. I picked up his trail here but I never saw him. Padre did. So did Brother Jude."

Mangel came over and licked Carlos's hand. The first flakes of snow landed on his head.

"God's messenger? Is that you, boy?"

Carlos held Mangel's head in his hands and began to cry.

"I won't go back to Sonora. The ranch is gone. Mother's dead. Felix—Mickey—I don't know him anymore, if I ever did. I'm sure he doesn't know me. Mickey Free. I wonder if he's free. What about you, Billy?"

"Right now my plan is to find us a rabbit."

A while later I was back with a pair of jacks. They were easy to find in the snow. Carlos had a fire going. We skinned and cleaned the jacks and skewered them on a metal spit, one of the few things the Comanches didn't take. It wasn't a great supper but we felt better. We didn't talk much. We were exhausted. Mangel cleaned up the leftovers while I laid out my bedroll. Mangel and me crawled in. Carlos stayed up and kept the fire going. I slept through the night for the first time since we'd been back.

Carlos left out at first light for the Tinde village. I stayed to keep an eye on things, but there wasn't much to look after. What the Comanches didn't burn they took. California was strong on my mind but I'd never had a compadre like Carlos. In truth I wasn't ready to leave. I figured on seeing what Carlos'd do before making my own plans. Sounded like he'd forsaken his vows. If he wanted revenge I was game. The monks were my amigos too.

I spent most of the day hunting. Shot a mule deer in early afternoon as it was crossing the sagebrush. Mangel was off hunting on his own. As I was dressing out the deer Mangel showed up. I cut a slice of brisket and tossed it to him. He ignored it. His hackles were up.

"What's the matter, boy? Comanches? Ole Moze?"

I picked up my Winchester. I was in the open. An easy target. Mangel was watching a nearby mesa. It was broken into side canyons, any one of which could hide unwelcome company. The rest of the terrain was sagebrush at least a quarter of a mile in any direction. If I headed across the open range, away from the danger, I'd be going away from the monastery and would have no cover if something or someone came after me. If I walked toward the mesa I'd be headed back to the monastery, but I might walk into an ambush.

Something for sure was out there and it was near the mesa. Mangel's hackles didn't lie. I flipped a coin in my head. Moze should have been denned up for the winter but I was betting on him. As much as I didn't want to meet him I figured he was better odds, especially if I was in the open. I hacked off a hindquarter and headed away from the mesa, leaving the rest of the deer behind. A hundred paces out I heard something tear into the meat. It woofed like a grizzly. Mangel had stopped growling but his hackles were still up. I wasn't about to run. Wouldn't look back neither. Staring down a grizzly can be dangerous as running from one. Another hundred paces and I looked sideward over my shoulder. It was a grizzly alright. It was huge.

It was evening when I got back to the monastery. Carlos was sitting by a fire on the plaza.

"I hope you brought supper," he said. "I've been nursing this fire the past few hours. Nearly gave up. You get the next load of wood."

His tone didn't sound like Brother Charles.

"Lord Grizzly wanted our supper. I gave him the biggest part and took a longer route home."

"Moze?"

"He was big enough. Right color too. How was your visit?"

"Not good. I spoke with the Tinde chief. He knew about the massacre. Said it was six warriors. He knows where they are but he won't go after them."

"Why not?"

"Didn't say. I think he doesn't want to start a war over a dead orphan. Not a war with Comanches."

"Did he say where they were?"

"Ojo Caliente."

"Where's that?"

"It's a cluster of hot springs on the road from Abiquiu to Taos. Two to three days walk from here. Indians consider it sacred for its healing waters. They set aside their differences—weapons too—while they're there."

"Good. Let's hope the devils hang around a few more days. If they've laid down their weapons, we'll make quick work of them."

"You think we should kill them?"

"Damn right! When Dolan's men killed John Tunstall we went after them. Didn't get all of them, but we got some. An eye for an eye and a tooth for a tooth."

"Jesus said to turn the other cheek. Leviticus says don't take revenge against the sons of your people."

"Fine words, but more than our cheeks have been slapped. And those sonsabitches ain't the sons of our people. I figure the Bible is okay with us pumping lead into their ugly asses. It's full of that kind of mayhem."

Carlos smiled. It was good to see some of the strain lift from him.

He'd been poking at the fire while we talked. Daylight was going fast. It was time to get the meat going if we were to eat before the cold turned bitter. I cut off the rump from the hindquarter and roasted it on the metal spit. When it was cooked we ate in silence. After dinner I cut thin slices from the rest of the hindquarter and salted them down. While I was smoking them Carlos finally spoke.

"Okay, Billy, pumping lead it is."

"You serious?" I figured I was being hornswoggled.

"I am."

"You've been thinking about this."

"Every waking minute."

"If we find them without weapons, you're okay about killing them, even though the springs are supposed to be sacred, a safe harbor?"

"The monastery was supposed to be a safe harbor."

"What would Padre Romuald think?"

"He's dead."

"Suppose he wasn't?"

"You know what he'd think."

"You ever kill a man?"

"No."

"You take the Winchester. I've got my six-shooter. There are six of them. I won't miss."

CHAPTER 22 **Brother Jude**

It's terrifying how quickly a grizzly can cover a short distance—terrifying when you consider how vulnerable you are if he turns toward you.

—BROTHER CHARLES, *Diary*, JUNE 3, 1875

THE TINDE CHIEF SAID THE Comanches would probably stick around the hot springs another week. That didn't give us much time. We allowed ourselves one more day smoking deer meat before skinning out for the springs.

While I was smoking jerky the next morning a raven landed a few paces away. He stared at the meat. I lifted off a piece and cut it into small strips. Tossed him one. He caught it and flew into a nearby cottonwood. A few minutes later he was back. Mangel was watching from across the plaza where he was sunning hisself. He ambled over. The raven flew into the tree. I tossed Mangel a bite. He snapped it up and lay down on his belly. Threw him a second bite. He caught it midair. The raven dropped out of the tree a couple of paces away. I tossed him a bite. Mangel lunged but the raven was quicker. When I threw a piece short of Mangel, the raven lunged but Mangel was quicker. The game was on.

After I stopped tossing strips, Mangel and the bird faced each other, squared off like fighters. Mangel laid his front legs on the dirt and jacked his butt in the air, challenging the raven to a new game. The raven hopped a few feet into the air. Mangel leapt to the side. The raven swooped toward Mangel's tail. Mangel spun around to meet him. I watched them play, then rewarded them with more strips of meat.

"What have we here?" Carlos asked as he came over to watch.

"I ain't sure. Señor Cuervo's taken a shine to Mangel. We may of found us another companion."

"He's a wolfbird," Carlos said. "He and Mangel are bonding. Question is, is he a manbird?

I didn't sleep well that night. Had another dream about Aunt Cat. A raven and her were playing fetch. She'd throw out a nut. Raven'd fly after it. When he found it he'd eat it, then fly back. This went on a bit. Finally Aunt Cat threw a nut so hard it kept on sailing. The raven flew after it and disappeared in the distance.

A light snow was falling when we awakened at first light. Señor Cuervo'd been waiting in a cottonwood. After he dropped down to the plaza I tossed him strips of deer meat while me and Carlos and Mangel finished off the rump roast from the night before. I told Carlos about my dream. Asked him what he thought about it.

"We talked about ravens being a symbol of death. For Apaches and for you. We've got killing in our hearts. I'm guessing that's what your dream is about. Someone is disappearing. But is it Comanches, or us?"

We finished breakfast, then packed up and left the monastery. The raven flew ahead.

"What are you naming him?"

"Brother Jude."

"Suppose he's a she?"

"Sister Judy."

We didn't see much of Brother Jude that morning. The sun was high by the time we reached the Spanish Trail. We turned east toward Abiquiu. The snow was mostly gone. A few patches hung around the north sides of mesas. When we stopped to eat, my new compañero showed up.

"I thought he might've gone home by now," Carlos said.

"He'll stick around as long as I feed him," I said, more out of hope than conviction.

After we ate we continued down the Spanish Trail. Brother Jude flew off again.

"Why you figure Brother Jude was half out of the ground?" I asked, thinking about the raven's namesake.

"Been wondering that myself. Looks like they roped him to a horse and ripped his head off. I'm guessing the other monks were screaming. Not Jude. He was the toughest of us. His silence probably enraged them."

A few minutes later Brother Jude landed in a piñon beside the trail, exercising a considerable vocabulary.

"Your compañero's trying to tell us something."

"Where's Mangel?" I said.

I leveled my Winchester. We stopped walking. Visibility was good. A few junipers but mostly sagebrush. Some of the sagebrush was tall as a man. If trouble was near it was well hidden. I called out to Mangel. In a few minutes he slunk out of the sagebrush. His eyes were large, his ears back, his lips tight against his teeth. The hairs on his spine from the withers to his tailbone were erect.

"Let's hold up a bit," I said. "Mangel's about as bad upset as I've seen. If trouble's out there let's give it time to move on."

I gave Carlos my Winchester. We stood back to back. I rested my hand on my six-shooter. Brother Jude kept up the racket, then went silent. Mangel's hackles settled and he was standing more upright. A few minutes later Brother Jude flew off. Mangel headed back into the sagebrush. Carlos handed me the Winchester.

"You keep it," I said. "Our compadres want us to be more vigilant."

We continued on toward Abiquiu, walking in silence. Dust devils rose on the trail ahead in the late-afternoon sun and spun toward the canyon walls. I was surprised because I'd only seen them before in the summer.

"I'm still wrestling with this love-thy-neighbor notion," I said when we started talking again. "If I found one of them Comanche devils helpless in a ditch I'd cut out his eyes and chop off his privates before putting a bullet in him. Not a moment's hesitation. You don't feel that? Even a little?"

"In God's eyes the Comanches are our neighbors. But there's the question of justice. That's a separate issue."

At heart Carlos was a gentle man. Everything about him was against killing. He was a crack shot with a rifle, but he told me once that the last thing he killed was an antelope, when he was fourteen. Did it only to feed his family. He ate meat if he had to but he ate beans and corn and greens when he had a choice. If he found varmints in the monastery he'd chase them out. He wouldn't kill them. He'd done an about-face after the massacre though. He was moody and withdrawn.

"I don't know what to tell you about justice," he said. "I've always known there was evil in the world. But nothing prepared me for the brothers buried to their necks in that fire pit. Their contorted faces. What was left of them."

The Spanish Trail followed along the Río Chama. At times the trail was beside the Chama. Other times the river was a quarter of a mile away across the sagebrush flats. The canyon walls rose on both sides, sometimes several dozen feet, sometimes several hundred. We were entering an area where the closed-in walls were hidden in shadows when Brother Jude flew toward us screaming.

He was too late. The grizzly was quick behind him. He was huge. Bigger than any grizzly I'd ever seen before or since. He looked near as tall as me when he was charging. Must of weighed every bit as much as Buck. Buckskin colored, streaked with gray. Figured it must be Moze.

He covered the distance near as fast as I could draw, his head barely off the ground. He was snorting, his ears laid back, his jaws popping like a six-shooter. I got off two rounds before he hit me. Carlos was behind me. Don't know if he got off any. The grizzly went right over me and into Carlos. I hit the ground flat on my back. My six-shooter flew into the sagebrush. I rolled over, gasping for air. When I looked up, the grizzly had Carlos on the ground. Carlos's head was in the bear's mouth.

I didn't see a gun anywhere. I pulled out my knife and I leapt on the bear's back, driving the blade into his hump. Hoped to hit the neck but couldn't reach far enough.

The grizzly dropped Carlos and reared up, flipping me off. I tried to scrabble backward but he swatted me across the chest with a paw the size of my head. He grabbed me by the butt in his jaws as I rolled over, trying to stand. I figured my luck had left me. He was shaking me like a willow branch when Mangel crashed through the sagebrush, sinking his teeth into the nearest hind leg. The grizzly dropped me and spun around. Mangel leapt backward and attacked from behind again. I glanced at Carlos. He'd rolled onto his side. The Winchester was under him. I grabbed it and emptied the magazine into the grizzly's head. Don't know how many rounds I fired but the grizzly fell with the third or fourth. Mangel turned loose when I levered the last case from the chamber. It was Moze alright. He was missing toes on his front foot.

My vest was ripped to flitterjigs. My chest was furrowed like a plowed field. Blood was flooding my pants from ugly gashes in my butt and legs. But as near as I could tell nothing was broken. Carlos was a different case. His head looked like it'd been in a hay press. One eye was gone. His nose was hanging by a thread. His jaw was crushed. At first I thought he was dead. I took off my shirt to clean his wounds and stop the bleeding. After I'd wiped off the blood, his teeth showed through his cheek. I got most of the bleeding stopped, then wrapped his head in my shirt, covering all but his good eye. The rest of him was okay.

When he came around he tried to pull the shirt off his head but I stopped him. He didn't know why his head was wrapped like a mummy.

"What happened?"

The words came out but they didn't sound like Carlos. They gurgled up from his belly, barely coherent. Blood clotted the shirt where his mouth should have been.

"Ole Moze. Mangel saved us."

"How bad is it?"

Carlos held his jaw, more to free his speech than to assess the damage. His words were slow. He seemed no more upset than if he'd broke a finger.

"Moze gnawed on your head. You're chewed up pretty good. How you feeling?"

“My jaw’s shattered. Except for this head wrap, I don’t feel much of anything.”

“You will. Need to get you to a sawbones quick. Can you walk?”

“I think so.”

I helped Carlos stand, then I looked in the sagebrush for my six-shooter. I recovered it and my knife and I reloaded my Winchester. Mangel was nosing around my pack. I pulled out a strip of jerky and gave it to him. I looked around for Brother Jude but he was nowhere in sight.

“You did good, boy,” I said as I rumpled Mangel’s head. “Stay close.”

My leg was stiff but I could walk. Carlos could walk too, at least for a bit. We looked like a pair of ragged wraiths too long in a coffin as we headed down the road to Abiquiu.

CHAPTER 23 **Ojo Caliente**

Treat every living soul with kindness.
Life is harder for them than you can imagine.

—BROTHER CHARLES, *Diary*,
THE SOLEMNITY OF ST. BENEDICT, 1880

THEN WE GOT A BREAK. We hadn't gone far when we met a patrol from the Abiquiu garrison. Carlos was light-headed and in pain and couldn't of walked much farther. It was getting dark and we'd of had to camp soon. I doubted Carlos would make it through the night. I told the troopers about the fight with Ole Moze. A few stayed with us while the rest rode back to the post to get a wagon.

The moon was rising when the wagon arrived. Carlos had blacked out. Soldiers lifted him into the back and me and Mangel crawled in beside him.

During the ride I mentioned the massacre. Carlos's head was wrapped and no one recognized him, but when I said "Brother Charles" a couple of troopers knew the name. I told them I was Bill Roberts. Figured they might know the name Billy Bonney.

We hadn't gone far when the ruts in the road shook Carlos awake. His pain was bad and he could barely talk, but he didn't seem to mind. I told him about my new name. He nodded and patted me on the knee.

Then he said, "When Moses led the Israelites to freedom he begged

God to show him his glory. God told him no man can see his face and live. Billy, I have seen the face of God. Moze set me free."

The moon was near its zenith when we arrived at the post. It wasn't much. Four log buildings, a stockade, a couple of dozen men. No doctor. The nearest in Santa Fe. Carlos could be there in two days in an ambulance. I feared he wouldn't survive the trip but it wasn't like we had a choice.

A couple of troopers bundled him into an ambulance and took off for Santa Fe. I couldn't chance going with him. Besides, I had work to do.

The officer in charge was Captain James Boyer. Most of his career was fighting Indians. Snakes, Yavapai, Sioux, Chiricahua. He knew you. Who you were anyway. He didn't know Carlos but he knew the abbot and Brother Jude. I told him Carlos was your brother. He figured me for a flannelmouthed liar, but when I described the massacre he sobered. I told him the Comanches were holed up at Ojo Caliente. He said he'd send a detail to round them up. That was good news. I told him I'd go with them. He said no, but I said that the butchered monks were my amigos, I had a horse to recover, and I was going regardless. The next morning me and eight troopers saddled up for the hot springs.

Before we left, Captain Boyer reminded us of the prohibition against fighting at the springs. He said the land was sacred and we should honor it. The loss of face with friendly tribes was too high a price. We were to bring the Comanches back alive if possible. Sergeant Macgregor was in charge. Macgregor assured the captain we'd respect the custom.

"Stay out of the way, Roberts," Captain Boyer called as we rode off. "Let Sergeant Macgregor handle this."

Mangel started to follow us. I rode back to the post and gave him to a corporal who said he'd tie him up until we returned.

By early afternoon we were within half a mile of the hot springs. We left the road and turned up an arroyo along the backside of a ridge leading past the springs. We tied up our horses and walked in silence the last hundred paces to the top of the ridge. Below was a Comanche kohgwa in a grove of cottonwoods. A ridge blocked their view of the settlement. Four of the devils were sitting around a campfire. A fifth, the biggest Indian I've ever seen, was returning from a string of ponies grazing in the high grass beside the spring. He was wearing a black monk's robe. Around his waist was a belt holding a sword and scabbard. The robe would of reached the ankles of any of the brothers but it didn't much more than cover his knees. We squatted below the ridgeline.

"It's them," I said. "The sword that big bastard's wearing cut off the abbot's hand."

"We can't attack here," Sergeant Macgregor said. "You heard the captain. 'Tis sacred ground."

"Sacred, my ass! The monastery was sacred."

Macgregor was a round-faced pudgy Scot with a big heart but not a thought in his brain. I marveled that Boyer'd picked him to lead the detail.

As the troopers talked tactics I heard a familiar nicker. Peered over the ridge and saw the sixth Comanche riding Buck. He was coming up a path from the settlement. I slipped over the ridge and worked my way down an arroyo. When I was within fifty paces I raised up with my Winchester and blew him off Buck. Then I raced toward the camp firing my six-shooter. The Comanche strutting in the black robe fell first. Three more fell in the next twenty paces. The last devil got to a rifle leaning against a tree and turned to face me when I plugged him twice, once in the chest, once in the forehead. The troopers dropped to the ground when the firing began. By the time the sergeant stormed over the ridge I was nuzzling Buck.

"Roberts! What in hell!"

"I plum lost my head," I said, trying to mollify Sarge.

"You done it now. The last thing Captain Boyer said was don't crap on the sanctity of this piss pot."

"If we hightail it now no one'll know who done it."

"You think they won't find us? They'll hunt us through eternity."

He was right. I've knowed Indians to track a man across the malpais.

"Your horseshoes don't say US Government," I said. "If we split up they won't know which way we went."

I jumped on Buck and raced toward the mustangs. Macgregor waved his men back over the ridge. The mustangs'd scattered like quail when the shooting started. When I had most of them I herded them through the woods where the troopers had been. I fired my six-shooter a couple of times and the mustangs raced toward the hot springs road with Buck and me close behind.

Buck ran hard, passing the mustangs, hardly slowing till we got to the Abiquiu road. We turned east and headed toward Santa Fe. After we'd gone far enough to mix our tracks in the maze of other hoofprints, we headed back toward the post. I doubted I was fooling anybody but at least I had something to throw at Captain Boyer while he was roasting me.

Mostly I was satisfied at the way things turned out. If Carlos was alive I hoped he'd get some peace if he knowed the killers were dead. At least I figured they were. In the confusion I hadn't checked. A mistake but I wasn't going to chew myself over it. Had a bad feeling all along about Carlos. He believed he should of died with the brothers. I figured there was a good chance he wanted the Comanches to kill him. If that was his plan and the grizzly got him first, well, that was better in my book. Maybe in God's too.

While I was chewing this over I heard a raven overhead. I looked up and here he came, doing cartwheels and somersaults as he dropped out of the sky. I figured he might crash into me but he skittered off at the last minute. Then I heard Mangel barking. He was racing toward me, a short rope flapping behind him like a second tail.

I pulled up the reins and skidded off Buck. Mangel leapt and caught me in the chest as my boots hit the ground. The two of us fell to the dirt. If anyone'd seen us they'd of figured we were drunk. Mangel stood on my chest licking my face, pawing the ruts Moze'd clawed into my hide. My chest and butt were throbbing. I rolled onto my side. Brother Jude was jumping at the rope dragging behind Mangel as it made sidewinder tracks in the dirt. I'd swear he was laughing at us.

It was dark when we got back to the post. Captain Boyer asked about Macgregor and his troopers. I told it like it was. If I'd downplayed it Macgregor would of made it worse when Boyer questioned him later that evening. I told Boyer I lost my head when I saw that devil riding Buck, but he saw through me.

"When you rode out of here I knew I should've thrown you in the stockade."

He was right of course. There wasn't much the captain could do but order me off the post. If I ever came back, he said he'd have me shot. I left about the time Macgregor showed up. Told him he might want to let Boyer cool off before he reported in.

Next morning I went to Gonzales's and bought a few supplies. I told the storekeep about the massacre and the fight with Moze. Believe he was partial to the bear. I said I was staying nearby a few days and asked him to tell me if he heard anything about Brother Charles. He knew all the monks. Couple of days later he told me your brother died on the way to Santa Fe.

In my heart I already knew it. I was thankful Carlos hadn't been at the hot springs. I was comfortable with the killing. It would be on my head. Carlos was different. He had a powerful conscience. If he'd knowed about the killing, he might of felt as much responsibility as if he'd pulled the trigger. But I wondered if Carlos'd somehow knowed. Maybe that's what really killed him.

CHAPTER 24 Amigos Perdidos

What you truly love will always be with you. Nothing else really matters.

—BROTHER CHARLES, *Diary*, OCTOBER 10, 1876

AFTER CARLOS DIED I WENT back to the monastery and laid up a few days to keep vigil over the brothers. Figured it's what Carlos would of done. The toolshed was the only building that hadn't burned. It would keep out the weather. The cot in Padre Romuald's room survived. I moved it to the toolshed. The Comanches piled most of the furniture and things in the church and set it afire, but they left a retablo of St. Anselm that Brother Thomas had painted. It was still hanging behind the alcove where the monks sat. It hadn't been scorched. I took it to the toolshed and hung it above the cot.

Took me a week to clean up the debris. I raked the rubble out of the buildings and burned it. What didn't burn I buried. Even the ashes. The Comanches'd burned most everything, including Brother Charles'—Carlos's—books. The only books that survived were his diary and a science book by an Englishman, Charles Darwin. Carlos's tin of Ceylon tea survived the fire too.

I leveled the ground where the monks had been burned, raking it and sweeping it with a broom of pine branches. The monastery was a ruin but most signs of the massacre were gone. Mother Nature would grind off the rough edges throughout the winter. If other monks ever wanted it they could build it back.

I hunted to feed me and Mangel and Brother Jude. Went to Abiquiu twice. Bought cartridges, coffee, flour, frijoles. A saddle and saddlebags. I had no money of my own but I'd found some pesos in Padre's room. He kept them in a small metal box in his closet. Surprised the Comanches missed it.

The storekeep at Gonzales's said a couple of Kiowas showed up asking questions a few days after the killing. I ran into Sergeant Macgregor on the second visit. He wasn't sore at me but he said I should avoid Captain Boyer. He said another band of Comanches had jumped the reservation and were in the area. Soldiers were looking for them. Said I should lay low, not tell anyone I was at the monastery. That was good advice. Wished I'd heard it earlier. It was time to leave.

When I went back to the monastery to gather my gear I cleaned out the toolshed and burned all sign of my presence. The only things I kept were Brother Thomas's retablo of St. Anselm, Carlos's diary, his tin of tea, and the science book. I walked Buck to the Chama. Tied him to the willows, then went back for a last look. I swept the tracks on the monastery grounds and the trail leading to the river. Another rain or snow would wash out most of the evidence that we'd been there. Buck and me waded into the Chama and headed toward the Spanish Trail. Brother Jude flew on ahead. Mangel followed.

When we reached the Spanish Trail we turned toward Abiquiu. If the Comanches were looking for me, losing my tracks in Abiquiu was my best move. I wasn't ready to head to California. Too much on my mind. I wasn't safe in New Mexico. Garrett gave me a break at Fort Sumner. He wouldn't do it again. I also had the Comanches to consider. They'd be out for revenge. They'd find someone to skin and I didn't plan on it being me.

I was uneasy about Macgregor. Comanches might go after the Abiquiu garrison. The more I thought about it, the more likely it seemed. But the soldiers were looking for Comanches too so I let it go.

By the time I got to Abiquiu I'd made up my mind. I decided to check on Juan Mundo, the di-yin who'd cured my hydro. I'd been to the Tinde village enough times to make friends with Juan. Frankly, I was worried about him. The night before, I had another dream about my

Aunt Cat. She was talking to Juan when I rode up. She looked at me and smiled, then she turned back to Juan. It was not like the bad dreams, the ones when someone dies. There were no ravens. Still it gnawed at me. So I figured to go to the Tinde village in case Juan got into trouble. It wasn't the best decision. Getting out of the territory was smarter, but anything was smarter than hanging around Abiquiu.

I dismounted, picked up Mangel, and climbed back in the saddle. Buck's hoofprints were similar to other hoofprints but Mangel had a cattywampus gait. His tracks'd be evident to a good tracker. He wasn't happy about riding on a saddle horn but he didn't argue none. The four of us—me, Buck, Mangel, and Brother Jude—headed into the mountains.

The Tinde village was two day's ride. Juan Mundo was glad to see me. I told him I'd had a dream about him.

"I know," he said. "I've been waiting for you."

He invited me to stay. He was an old man. He'd been on the Long Walk but he held no bitterness toward Americans. Mangel and me shared a grass bed covered with wapiti hides in his tepee. I fed Brother Jude every morning. He could scavenge for hisself but I figured feeding him would keep him around.

Spent the winter with Juan. We had two heavy snows that year. One storm dumped snow up to my waist. I hunted throughout the winter, mostly for wapiti and deer. As soon as the weather warmed, Juan wanted to collect eagle feathers. On top of a nearby cliff was a cleft barely big enough to hold a man. Juan laid branches across the slit, then returned a few times over the next week, leaving freshly killed rabbits on the branches. One morning before sunup he slipped into the cleft. Within an hour an eagle came to inspect the kill. It made several passes before settling down for breakfast. While the bird was ripping apart the rabbit, Juan reached through the branches, grabbing the legs and wrapping them with a leather thong. With the eagle tethered, Juan plucked three tail feathers. When he released the bird he waited till it was out of sight before he climbed out. I've seen an eagle bring down an antelope. Believe it could kill a man if it took a notion.

A few weeks later I was hunting wapiti in the Brazos and came upon fresh lion tracks. A dusting of snow had fallen the night before. I was riding Buck. Mangel and Brother Jude were with me. Mangel recognized the tracks and took off. Me and Buck followed. Before long Mangel treed the lion in a large spruce. When we rode up, the lion sprang from the tree and disappeared over a cliff, with Mangel and Brother Jude quick behind him. Mangel's barking shifted to a wail.

When I got to him his face was ripped open from the top of his skull to his jaw. The brain case was broken. He'd fallen a good fifty feet. His bad leg was twisted beneath him, the bone exposed in three places. He lay on his side whimpering. Brother Jude was standing by his head squalling. Mangel looked at me with those soft black eyes. Then he stopped whimpering. I stepped behind him so he couldn't see and pulled out my six-shooter. Brother Jude flew into a nearby tree shrieking like a banshee when I pulled the trigger.

I wrapped Mangel in my blanket and lifted him onto the saddle horn. Buck didn't balk. I swung into the saddle. We were a few hours from the monastery. I rode back with Brother Jude circling high overhead, still shrieking. When we got to the monastery I dug a grave next to Scout. I laid Mangel in the ground, wrapped in my blanket. I was wearing the Apache charm that a Mescalero squaw gave to Dick Brewer for saving her life. I laid it on top of the blanket.

"Goodbye, old friend. You were the best. This charm didn't help Dick none but maybe it'll help you on the journey home. It may of saved my neck a time or two but you were my true good luck charm. The blanket'll keep you warm. I won't forget you. Ever."

I filled in the grave, then covered it with stones. When I'd finished I fashioned a cross from pine wood and fixed it in the ground. I spent the night sleeping beside Mangel's grave. Awoke two or three times to a line from the psalms the brothers often sang: "I lie in the dust of death with dogs all around me."

Next morning, after cleaning up my sign, I said goodbye to Mangel and left for the Tinde village. Brother Jude was in a piñon beside Mangel's grave when I rode away. Carlos was right. He was a wolfbird. Between

Brother Jude and Aunt Cat, ravens had been my totem. I hung around the Tinde village a few days, hoping Brother Jude'd return, but it was time to go.

During long winter evenings Juan had taught me about the Tinde way of life. He said all paths lead to the same spring and I should follow the path I knew best. Next morning me and Buck headed for California.

CHAPTER 25 **Billy the Kid**

The Kid's body lies undisturbed in the grave—
and I speak of what I know.

—PAT GARRETT, *The Authentic Life of Billy the Kid*

CALIFORNIA WAS BETTER AND WORSE than I expected. Got a job on a ranch outside of Los Angeles working cattle and horses. Met a girl. My boss had a library. I read for hours of an evening. Learned how to tend orange groves. Grew a beard and went near bald on top. One day reading the *Los Angeles Times* I learned that Colonel Roosevelt was recruiting cowboys. To free Cuba from the bonds of Spain, the paper said. He would be in San Antonio in a few weeks. I barely knew where Cuba was but the idea of one last adventure warmed my blood.

Over the years I'd had pangs about abandoning Paulita. The baby too. Maybe it wasn't too late to right things. Could go to Texas and Cuba, then back to Fort Sumner to pick up where I'd left off with her.

You're right. It was a foolish notion.

After fifteen years I'd seen enough of California. The ocean's stark and beautiful. The mountains are sprawling ranges, some as big as any in Colorado. And the redwoods are twice the size of ponderosas and firs in the Sacramentos. But California has temblors. Buck and me got caught in one. We were hunting javelina in Baja when a temblor hit. We got thrown. Buck broke a leg, I broke a shoulder. Had to put him down. Hadn't been for the boys with me I might of hung it up in Baja.

Wished I could of brought Buck back to the monastery. Lay him beside Mangel.

Temblors rolled in for weeks afterward. One hit Los Angeles the day I was reading about Cuba. I quit my job, said goodbye to my girl, and headed for Texas.

It was spring of '98 when I got back on the Spanish Trail, riding a bay named Maddie. Didn't expect to run into trouble in New Mexico. The Lincoln County War was ancient history. Figured nobody much cared anymore. Or even remembered Billy Bonney. With my age and whiskers I figured even my old compadres wouldn't recognize me. I was wearing these specs too. Too much reading in dark rooms.

The trail was worse than I remembered. Sometimes there was no trail at all. Up in Utah I rode through Mountain Meadows, site of a Mormon massacre thirty years earlier. It was a five-day battle, like the one that ended the Lincoln County War. Over a hundred emigrants were killed. I'd missed it on the way west and might of missed it on the way back if Maddie hadn't kicked up a skull. Found other bones and parts of old wagons. After the monastery I had a darker view of what the emigrants'd been through.

A month and a half out of Los Angeles I stopped at the Tinde village where I'd stayed the winter I lost Mangel. My old compañero Juan Mundo was the only one left. He was ancient. He told me a band of Comanches hiding out in the San Juans had attacked the village after I left. The survivors moved to the Tierra Amarilla reservation. Comanches also attacked the post at Abiquiu. They snuck in before daylight while soldiers were asleep. Killed over half the garrison. Juan said they were avenging the killing of six of their own at Ojo Caliente. I asked him how the Comanches fingered the soldiers. He said some Kiowas were camped at the springs. One of the Comanches was still alive when they showed up.

I didn't say nothing. I'd told Juan about the killing right off when it happened. He might of held me responsible for the attack on his village. Or maybe he was old and had forgotten.

A few days later I stopped at the monastery. It'd changed some. The roofs had fallen in on near every building. The front wall of the church was a pile of rubble. Piñons and junipers grew in the commons, blocking the view of the canyon walls across the way.

The graves were overgrown with weeds but they were still visible on a rise above the river. The crosses were rotted but the stones were there. I spent the better part of the afternoon at Mangel's grave. I told him about Buck. They weren't the best of friends but I figured he'd want to know. I talked about Moze too. If Mangel hadn't showed up when he did I wouldn't be telling this tale. I got the better half of that partnership.

It was early for wildflowers but I found some yellow columbines and laid them on his grave. I'd asked Carlos once about dogs in heaven. He figured that if there was a heaven, dogs had as much right to it as anybody and more right than most. It was heaven that he was less sure of. He talked about freedom and being fully alive instead. He told me once that he thought hell was more a state of mind than a real place. Believe he felt the same about heaven.

I put in a word for Mangel. Figured it couldn't hurt. I told him that if there was a heaven I'd look for his sign and I'd follow the tracks through eternity till I found him. I said a few words for Scout and the monks too. And Raúl. They'd given their lives to the monastery. They were all saints in my ledger.

I stayed the night at the monastery. The next day I rode into Abiquiu. Stopped by Gonzales's. A fellow named Bodie was running the store. I asked him what he knew about the Comanche raid. He said nobody talked about it much. No Comanches had been in the area in years. He didn't know what'd become of the raiding party. He didn't know any of the soldiers either. The army post was abandoned, that much he knew. Business had suffered some. Monks from back East had been to the monastery years earlier. Never came back.

Next morning I left for Santa Fe. Camped the night along the Río Grande and rode into town the next day. I'd planned to avoid the town but changed my mind. Santa Fe had grown some. I rode by the calaboose on Water Street. I'd spent three months there twenty years earlier, waiting for my trial. Wrote letters, three of them, to Governor Wallace while I was locked up. Trying to get amnesty. He didn't answer. Me and the boys tried to dig our way out. Got caught, of course. I spent the rest of the time chained to a post. That was the time I was sentenced to hang for killing Sheriff Brady. That was one killing I didn't do. But I've already told you that.

I stopped at the Exchange Hotel for dinner. A cockfight drew a crowd in the courtyard. The smell of blood was pungent. I'd washed dishes at the hotel when I was a kid and I knew that smell. Took my dinner outside. Passing a newsstand I saw a stack of books. On top was *The Authentic Life of Billy the Kid as told by Pat Garrett.*

I opened the book and began reading: "A true history of the life, adventures, and tragic death of William H. Bonney, better known as Billy, the Kid." Billy the Kid! There was a twist. And here I'd thought Billy Bonney was all but forgotten. I forked over three liberty nickels. Soon as I finished dinner I opened the book again. By the end of the day I'd learned that Garrett's Billy had killed twenty-one men during his twenty-one years. He was born in New York City. His mother was Catherine McCarty. The family lived in Coffeyville, Kansas. Sounded like Garrett'd confused me with Bob Dalton. The story continued with more foolishness.

Where'd he come up with this sheep-dipper, I wondered. His Billy was a mix of me, Kid Antrim, Jesse Evans, and a drunken imagination. It was full of surprises. The title said the story was about Billy Bonney but Pat Garrett was the hero. I figured old Pat was on hard times if he was writing a book about his own antics. It gave me a good laugh but it had a serious downside. Billy Bonney was back in the news. Figured I'd better get out of Santa Fe straight off and stay clear of towns big enough for newsstands. I started to stick the book in my saddlebag but decided to leave it on the plaza. I didn't want to be carrying hints of my former life.

Garrett was still making trouble for me.

A few days later I pulled up at a ranch outside Fort Sumner. Didn't recognize it and figured the owner wouldn't know me. Jacob Spiegelberg met me at the door. Invited me in for breakfast. He was German. He'd lived there about ten years. I introduced myself as Bill Roberts. Told him I'd once spent some time in Fort Sumner. Jacob knew Pete Maxwell. Said Pete was still alive but no one had seen him in years.

"Why's that?"

"When Sheriff Garrett shot Billy Bonney, Herr Pete was scared. Neighbors heard him scream. Afterward folk addressed him as Don Shootme."

"I recall Pete had a sister. Pauline?"

"Paulita. She married and moved to Mora."

"Paulita. That's it. Married? Does she have any kids?"

"Nein. She lost one many years ago."

"How's she doing?"

"Good I guess. I do not see her. She and Herr Pete had a fall out."

Jacob's wife fixed a delicious breakfast of huevos and chorizo. I ate till I about foundered. Offered to pay for the meal but Jacob wouldn't accept anything. I thanked them for their hospitality and made my goodbyes.

I steered clear of Fort Sumner and rode on to San Patricio, avoiding Lincoln too. I wanted to see María and Manuel. Paulita was my sweetheart and I've had other amantes, but María stole my heart. I've often regretted that she was married when I met her.

The Montoya choza was in ruins. The roof had holes big enough a cat could fall through. A crow flew out when I went to the door. I asked a neighbor what'd happened. She said that years earlier hombres had passed through looking for Manuel. María was home by herself. They hung her naked from a cottonwood and set the furniture on fire. Manuel came home that evening. He cut her down and buried her on a rise back of the house. Next morning he shot hisself beside the cottonwood. Neighbors buried him beside María.

I talked to other neighbors. None would admit to knowing anything. It happened so long ago they said. They'd never heard of Manuel being in trouble. I stayed in San Patricio a week but couldn't turn up a clue. I visited María's grave one last time and kissed the gravestone, then Maddie and me rode away.

I stopped off at John Tunstall's ranch on the Feliz. It had a new house, a nice adobe place. John's old choza was barely standing. A family named Holmes was staying in the new house. They offered me dinner and a bed for the night. They told me the story of John's killing. One of John's hands, Billy Bonney, had stolen horses from Jimmy Dolan. Bonney brought the horses to John's ranch. When Dolan found out, he sent a posse after them. John took the horses into the mountains to hide them. When the posse caught up with him they killed him.

Next morning I thanked the Holmes and left. I wondered if I should ride to Las Cruces. It wasn't on the way to San Antonio but Pat Garrett was sheriff of Dona Anna County and I halfway wanted to see him. I was curious about what happened at Fort Sumner, especially after reading Pat's version. And Pat might know something about María and Manuel.

Pat and me had rustled cattle together on the south end of the Pecos. Always liked him. Didn't hold a grudge against him for hunting me like he done. Just doing his job. Never figured it was personal. But after all those years things might of changed. Maybe he'd convinced hisself *The Authentic Life* was true. If he knew I was alive, maybe he'd want to finish the job, quietly, so I wouldn't put the lie to his book. If I was to see him I'd have to be careful. He wouldn't risk a showdown but he might bushwhack me. In the end curiosity overcame my better sense. When I got to Las Cruces I stopped by his office. I walked in and took off my hat. Pat was sitting behind a desk, facing the door.

"Hello, Pat."

"What can I do for you, sir?"

"You don't remember me?"

Pat's right hand dropped below the desktop. He slowly slid open a drawer.

"Should I?"

"Billy Bonney. But I go by Bill Roberts now."

"Billy! My god!"

Pat rose from his chair and came around to grip my arm and shake my hand.

"My god! How the hell are you?"

"I'm good, Pat. I'm good."

"Here, grab a seat. My god, it's been a long time. Last I heard about you, you was skinning out for parts unknown, John Poe egging you on."

"Poe, huh? He was a hell of a shot. Took some of my teeth and plowed a furrow across my pate."

"Where've you been? Figured you left New Mexico. If you'd stuck around I'd of heard."

We went to a café for dinner and talked into the afternoon. I asked him about the old days.

"What was it all about, Pat—the Lincoln County War? Murphy, Dolan, Tunstall, McSween, you, me? All the killing?"

"Oh hell, Billy, it was what it's always about. Power and greed. You and me? We was just doing our jobs. That's all."

"Yeah. You're probably right . . . Hey, you remember that time we had our picture made in La Mesilla? With a couple of the boys?"

"I remember. Wilson and Kid. We were a scruffy bunch."

"You keep it?"

"Gave it to my oldest boy. A memento of Billy the Kid."

Pat told me about his stint with the Texas Rangers. He talked about the gunfight at Tascosa, Texas. Mostly over a girl. Bigger than the Earp brothers' gunfight in Tombstone he said. It happened after he moved back to New Mexico but he felt responsible. Believed if he'd stayed in Tascosa he could of kept the boys under control.

I told him about my time in California. Left out the monastery. Left out the Comanches. Mostly I painted a quiet life, staying out of trouble, tending cattle and orange groves. I showed him a Billy he'd never knowed. He laughed. Said he'd written about a Billy I never knowed.

Asked him if he knew anything about María and Manuel. Said he didn't.

"Hell, Pat, I never heard of hanging a woman."

"It's a terrible thing, Billy. Terrible. When'd it happened?"

"Maybe fifteen years ago."

"Nothing to be done about it. Mexicans are murdered all the time. Killers never caught. Nobody looks for 'em."

Eventually I asked Pat what really happened in Fort Sumner.

"Pretty much like it says in the book with a few adjustments here and there. Wasn't sure who I shot. You and Kid look alike in the dark. When I realized it was Kid, Pete and me talked it over. Him and Paulita were fine saying it was you. Paulita I think it was suggested it. No one wanted to see you dead. Leastways none of your amigos in Fort Sumner. They all figured it was a good way to get you out of the territory with your hide intact. The hombres we lined up for the autopsy took our word that it was you. Me and Ash Upson talked about writing the book. I knew a little of your history. Ash made up the rest. Said listing me as author would give the story *authenticity*. He put that word in the title."

"It's a lot of things, Pat, but authentic ain't one of them. Did Ash know it was Kid, not me?"

"Nah. No one knows. No one who wasn't there. Sure, we made up stuff. Had to to tell a good story. Did you like it?"

"I ain't your best reader."

"Me and Ash was broke. If they'd paid me for killing Kid like they was suppose to, we wouldn't of done it. How'd you like the part about twenty-one men? That was pure Ash. I wanted twenty-eight, one more than Wes Hardin. Twenty-seven's what the newspapers said about him. He claimed to of killed forty-two but that was a lie. You think we told some whoppers, you should read Wes's book. I figured twenty-eight would make you a legend. Ash was better at legending. Twenty-one was poetry. One for every year of your sad young life."

"You created a legend alright."

"Problem is nobody's bought it. Ash and me would of wound up in debtors' prison if they hadn't of changed the law. We thought we'd make us a fortune like Ned Buntline. Buntline made Bill Hickok and Bill Cody. 'Wild Bill' and 'Buffalo Bill'? That was Buntline. You being Billy, we figured you was already half legendary. Ash put you and Kid together, come up with 'Billy the Kid.' We figured Ash'd out-Nedded old Ned. He wrote one hell of a story. I've talked so much about it I pret near believe it myself. Don't know why it don't sell."

"Ash still around?"

"He died a few years back. Bad health. Too much alcohol. I took care of him some. Paid his saloon bills. Took him home some nights. Family wasn't too happy but what could I do? Buried him myself. He was a good man. Hell of a writer too. I hated losing him."

"How come you never got paid for killing Kid?"

"Needed a coroner's report. They was one but I lost it. I come up with another, put Xs for witnesses' signatures. They figured it was forgery."

"Didn't folks speak up about Billy the Kid being two hombres?"

"Hell, some of them newspapers'd already gotten you and Kid mixed up. Everybody was using an alias. It's a wonder the papers got anyone straight. Most folks who knew better wouldn't read the book. Those who might, who cares? Buntline trifled with the truth. No one objected as long as he told a good tale."

"Ash told a good one."

"What brings you back?"

"Cuba."

"Cuba?"

"Cuba. Uncle Sam's looking for volunteers to run off the Spanish."

"I heard. Some guy name Roosterfelt or Roostertail is recruiting in San Antone next month."

"It's been a long time since I've had a serious good time. Shooting Spaniards could be fine sport. Come with me."

"Me? No. I get seasick thinking about boats. No, Billy, you go free the heathens. Become a hero. *The Authentic Life* cost me nothing but money. Make a name for yourself in Cuba, maybe I'll turn a profit yet."

CHAPTER 26 **Cuba Libre**

I wish there was no fighting. I wish there was no war. I wouldn't take a thousand dollars for my experience, but I don't want five cents more.

—TROOPER BEN COLBERT, *Diary*, JULY 12, 1898

THREE WEEKS LATER I STOPPED at the Alamo. San Antonio had grown up around the old church since I was there. The church was in sadder shape than I remembered. I walked through it thinking about Travis and Bowie and Crockett holding off Santa Anna's federales for thirteen days. Two hundred men against two thousand. We could of used a few of those boys in Lincoln the day the army showed up with a Gatling gun and a howitzer.

I took a room in the Menger Hotel down the street from the Alamo. Next day I learned that San Antonio was a training ground, not a recruiting camp. Recruiting was elsewhere and it was over. Colonel Roosevelt had his men. Called them Rough Riders. Figured me and Maddie'd come two thousand miles for nothing. Was about to head out when I heard that a couple of boys'd skinned out shortly after showing up. I talked my way onto the training ground. After proving my skills with a gun and a horse I was the last recruit.

Two days later Colonel Roosevelt hisself showed. He was Secretary of Navy or some such thing and had recently been made a lieutenant colonel. He was an eastern gent but he'd been a rancher and lawman in the Dakota Territory. He knew something of the cowhands in town. The

Menger'd put up signs saying Roosevelt would meet recruits in the saloon that evening. As the saloon filled, the crowd spilled into the dining hall and out into the street. Cowhands were thirty or more deep around open windows.

Roosevelt told us the Cubans were fighting for freedom like the patriots at the Alamo. We remembered the Alamo he said. It was time to remember the *Maine*. That was the ship that started the war when it sank. He read Travis's letter addressed to the people of Texas and all Americans. Toward the end he paused to say that Travis was talking to us. Then he read the last lines: "If this call is neglected, I am determined to sustain myself as long as possible and die like a soldier who never forgets what is due to his own honor and that of his country. Victory or death." The crowd erupted in whoops of "Victory or death." Whiskey bottles hit the walls. Gunfire filled the night sky. The town was in riot. The party was still going when I passed out in the small hours.

Most of the recruits were skilled with hardware and horses. During the weeks of training it was the marching that was the biggest challenge. Roosevelt called me out one day for being out of step.

"Sorry, Colonel," I said. "I can step pretty good on a horse."

After a train took us to Florida we spent more weeks with other outfits, waiting. The boredom was torture, especially when it was rumored that we might not get to Cuba. Most of the Rough Riders were cowhands, prospectors, hunters. Hombres used to rough work and long hours, not idleness. Whiskey and card games and occasional fights were our chief entertainment. When the ships finally arrived they were short by half. Half the men and near all the horses would stay behind. My regiment was one of the lucky ones. I'd brought Maddie with me but I left her in Tampa. The army promised to look after her till I returned.

On board ship I met Jack Davis, a cowboy from Montana. About ten years older than me. He'd served under General Crook during the Sioux campaign. After Rosebud Creek he was headed to the Little Big Horn when Crook decided to give his boys a rest. Jack wished they hadn't. If

Crook had gone on they might of saved Custer. Or they might of been massacred. Jack missed army life and was glad to get one more shot at it.

Jack had with him a feist named Taco he'd picked up in Tampa. He was our regimental mascot. Some of the other regiments had mascots too. A prospector'd brought an eagle from Arizona. A cowboy brought a lion cub from New Mexico. Another roped a pig when we stopped at a siding in Alabama. Taco was the only mascot to make it to Cuba.

Halfway to Cuba we hit bad weather. Waves crashed over the deck. The ship rocked right angles from port to starboard and back. Most of the boys were sick. Horses too. The hold stank of vomit, piss, and shit. When we got to Cuba we were all green. A few horses had broke legs and had to be put down.

The Daiquirí harbor was beautiful the morning we arrived. Wide beaches lined with palm trees, mountains rising out back. The sea was swollen from the storm but the sky was clear. Sapphire like the sea. Like the skies in New Mexico. The swells were six to eight feet high. The landing boats and ships rocked in opposite directions. We had to jump to the boats as they came up and the ship went down. If we missed we might be crushed between the hulls. Men broke arms, legs. Two drowned. Weighted down with heavy loads, they sank like stones. Rescuers had to cut off their packs before hauling them to the surface.

Horses and mules had the worst of it. No landing boats for them. They were herded off the backs of ships and had to swim to shore. Some broke legs as they fell on top of one another. Some drowned. I was glad I left Maddie in Tampa. One string was headed for Florida till a bugler on shore got them turned around.

"Them's Seventh Cavalry stock," Jack said. "That ole boy's playing 'Garryowen.'"

Jack and Taco and me boarded the landing craft without mishap. We were carrying provisions for a couple of days. The rest of our provisions never arrived. Maybe lost at sea. Maybe never shipped. A Horseman of the Apocalypse had joined our regiment. We'd see the other three before we'd get home.

Daiquirí was a ghost town. Cubans ran off when the war started and the Spaniards left when our warships fired on them. We didn't stick around either. We headed for Siboney seven miles away. It was a rough slog, especially for the cowboys used to traveling on horseback. We marched through the mountains at a dogtrot with sixty-pound loads.

The island was a furnace. Not even the rain gave relief. Mosquitoes were the worst of it. Taco constantly snapped at the ones buzzing his face. Mosquitoes were in our eyes, our mouths. They swarmed our backsides when we dropped our drawers. One flew in my ear and tap-danced on my eardrum. That's as near crazy as I've ever been. Tried poking the little bastard with a twig. When that didn't work I tilted my head sideward and drowned it in gun oil.

Every man jack was exhausted when we settled in for the night at Siboney. Next morning half the men tossed their breakfasts. I had a headache. Jack had the running shits. We were headed to a mountain pass called Las Guásimas two hours away. Spaniards were waiting for us. Jack was in no condition to move but he was no quitter.

"Didn't come here to fall to fever," he said. "If I'm ending my days on this dunghill it's with a bullet. Help get me going, Bill."

I grabbed his gear and we set off after Roosevelt. Instead of taking the road from Siboney to Santiago, Roosevelt picked a cattle path through the jungle. Cuba is hilly country. The cattle path wandered through the worst of it. Between the heat and the sickness, the hills and the pace, troopers dropped like ticks off deer. If they weren't dropping theirselves they were dropping ponchos, tents, blankets, rations. Pretty much everything but carbines and ammunition. Jack could barely drag hisself. I gave him a hand over the worst of it. Troopers passed us as we pushed through the jungle. By the time we reached the hornets' nest at Las Guásimas we were at the back of the pack.

There was a large field in front of us. Spaniards in the jungle across the way were firing Mausers with smokeless powder, making them near invisible. The Mausers fired several rounds to every one from our Springfields and Krags. As lead whizzed overhead, leaves rained down like on a fall day. I left Jack and moved to the front, firing blind. When a troop of Rough Riders to my left charged across the field, the spooks materialized, exposing their backsides as they took to the hills. The fighting was over. It'd lasted a couple of hours.

Spaniards had heavy casualties. We lost a few. A few more were wounded. Major Alexander Brodie was one. Remember him in the Apache War? He remembered you. Thought you were one hell of a scout. Said you were half Mexican, half Irish, whole sonofabitch. He survived and was governor of Arizona Territory for a while.

After the fighting I went looking for Jack. He was lying on his back. Taco was curled up beside him.

"Slept through the skirmish," Jack said as he nodded toward Taco. "Not them buzzards. They've been eying us."

He raised his Krag and fired. A black bird dropped from the sky. The rest drifted over the ridge. Taco went over to investigate.

"Ain't that bad luck?" I asked.

"Bad luck for the bird," he said. "His own damn fault."

After weeks of training and days of idleness, sickness, and misery, the day ended in celebration. That night, while we were eating supper and after the whooping'd quieted, an Irish boy sang "The Vacant Chair."

We shall meet, but we shall miss him.
There will be one vacant chair.
We shall linger to salute him,
While we say our evening prayer.

The conversations within earshot dropped away. Even the crickets stopped calling. That ole boy could make a glass eye cry.

We held up for the next week, waiting for orders, surviving on guinea hens and land crabs. We shot the hens. The crabs hid in burrows but would come out when we tapped the ground. When it was time to move out, Jack's fever had passed. Mine was cranking up. My head was full of butterflies, my body was a furnace. Jack carried my gear. We spent the better part of the day slugging through the mud. The rain had stopped but the heat and humidity was like a sweat lodge. We spent the night camped in the tall grass beside the road, clutching whatever sleep we could. One of the buffalo soldiers next to us had dropped his blanket on the march to Las Guásimas. Jack split his blanket and gave half to the trooper.

Next morning I woke to shells exploding overhead. They were bad but the explosions in my head were worse. Shrapnel rained down on us. We scattered like quail behind a nearby hill, every man for hisself. The trooper who got Jack's blanket was ahead of me when he tumbled into the mud. When I got to him blood was gushing from his neck. I sliced a rag from his blanket and shoved it against the wound. As long as I pressed the rag against him the blood held. If I lifted the rag, blood spurted again. I called for a medic but no one came.

When the shelling stopped, troopers moved out. The buffalo soldier and me were the last to leave. I held onto him until a couple of medics finally showed. They wrapped his neck and put him on a litter. He raised his hand to me as they hauled him off.

I caught up with my regiment at the base of San Juan Hill. It was the last redoubt before Santiago. Horses pulling guns up the hill were raked by sniper fire. Those that survived rolled across the bodies of compadres. When I found Jack I told him his blanket may of saved a soldier's life.

A canebrake along the San Juan River blocked our route up San Juan Hill. To the right was a lower ridge we called Kettle Hill. It had a huge cast-iron sugar kettle on top. When bullets caromed off the kettle it rang like a bell. Our orders were to clear snipers from the hill and hold it. The problem was getting to the top alive. Hiding in the brakes was futile. We were turkeys in a shooting gallery.

Roosevelt was the only Rough Rider on horseback. He'd bought a bay in San Antonio. Named it Little Texas. Roosevelt rode among the troops cheering us on, blind to the bullets buzzing past.

"Shoot out their eyes, boys," he yelled. "You'll spoil their aim."

He caught some shrapnel once. That was it. Sniping at him was like shooting a spook. But troopers around him fell thick as autumn leaves. We might of all been killed if Sergeant Porter hadn't shown up with Gatling guns. The sound of guns spraying snipers at seven pops a second was as sweet as the patter of spring rain. Troopers cheered.

As Roosevelt rode past he roared, "Quit lollygagging, men. Charge!"

He spurred Little Texas toward the base of the hill. Troopers poured out of the brakes screaming like prophets of doom. Roosevelt ran into a fence halfway up the hill and leapt from Little Texas. Troopers caught up with him and raced one another to the top. Lobos swift to the kill. Snipers abandoned their hideouts and sprinted for the Spanish line.

"Backsides make good targets," Roosevelt roared. "Make every bullet count."

A sniper ran toward Roosevelt, waving a saber. The colonel leveled his Colt and fired. The sniper folded like a tent. By the time I reached the top of the ridge Rough Riders were whooping. Roosevelt was doing a war dance. Our boys had routed the Spanish from the ridge.

I looked for Jack but he wasn't around. I went back down the hill and found him snagged in the fence. A buzzard was eyeing him from a few paces away. Taco was standing between them, growling, his hackles up. I shot the buzzard. Taco went over to investigate. Jack lifted his head. I pulled him from the fence and laid him on the ground. Taco came back and licked his face. Jack smiled. His clothes were ripped. He was neck to knee in blood.

"I figured you for dead."

"Kindly figured so myself. This here's the worst of it."

He opened his jacket. He was gutshot.

"Hang on. I'll find a medic."

"Won't do no good, Bill. I'll be gone afore he gets here. Stay with me."

I sat down beside him, flipping away a land crab with my boot. The fever was kicking in. I closed my eyes to stop the fandango.

"Figured the odds when I signed up. It's alright. I've had close scrapes afore. One of 'em was bound to get me. War ain't a bad way to go. Something righteous about it. Beats the hell out of old age. Wished I was back in Montana though. Got a little ranch on the Musselshell. Fine cattle country. Sweet sweet grass. It's where I expected to end my days."

"I'll get you home if I have to carry you."

"Kindly offer, Bill, but you ain't in condition to carry your carbine. It'd be nice though to spend a few years in Montana watching my bones molder. Ever been to Montana?"

"No. Seen Colorado, Wyoming."

"If they's a God, Montana's where he'd hole up. You believe in God, Bill?"

"There's something out there," I said. "God's as good a name as any for it."

"My pappy was a preacher. I grew up with the Bible. Read it all my life. Can't say exactly why. Weird ain't it. Even carry the family Bible with me. Listen, I don't want you hauling my bones back to Montana, but I'd sure 'preciate it if you'd see that my daughter Rindy gets my Bible."

"Sure, Jack. Be honored to. "

"It's in my war bag. Rindy lives in Lavina, not far from my ranch. Send it to Clarinda Davis, Lavina, Montana. She'll get it. There ain't that many folks in Lavina."

"Jack, I—"

He was gone before I got out the sentence. I was looking across the way, watching boys die, and I didn't see the light leave his eyes. A fly flitted around his face, then settled on one of his eyes. I flicked it away and closed his lids.

I sat there a long time thinking about Jack and me and the boys across the way. I remembered one morning at the monastery when Padre Romuald was saying mass. About the time he lifted the communion wafer above his head and repeated the words of Jesus at the Last Supper the sun broke through a crack in the ridge across the way. The light came through a window and lit up the communion wafer and Padre's hands. Then something happened that's always haunted me. Padre hisself lit up. I don't mean the sun lit him up. I mean he was the light itself. He glowed like a lantern. He lit up the whole room. As the light from him flowed through me, I . . . I—I don't know—I somehow became one person with him. One with all the monks in the chapel. It was like I could feel their blood in my veins. The monks were my brothers. They were me. I was them. I loved them each and every one to the very core of my soul. Some of them I'd never even spoke to.

I didn't know what the hell had happened. I'd seen Sister Blandina glow like a torch—I told you about that—but I didn't feel the love from her like I did with the monks. I asked Brother Charles about it after mass. He said that Padre was a saint and I'd had a vision. He reminded me of a conversation we'd had earlier about loving your neighbor. He said he could explain only part of what it meant at the time because I wasn't ready.

Then he said, "Jesus didn't say love your neighbor as you love yourself. He said love your neighbor *as yourself.* As you. Like you and your neighbor are one and the same. Like you loved the monks when they were part of you."

I thought I'd understood what Brother Charles'd meant, but it wasn't until Kettle Hill that I figured it out. I realized then that war's a fools' game. We didn't belong there killing our brothers, killing a part of ourselves.

Years ago when I worked at Fort Grant—before I met you—an old Papago worked there. He spoke a little Spanish. I got to know him. He told me that when he was a boy about my age he killed a Pima, the only hombre he'd ever killed. He said that when a Papago kills someone, he goes through a healing ceremony to cleanse his soul. He stays away from his family until he has a vision. Before he goes home he turns his vision into a song. I asked him about his vision song. He sang it for me in Papago, then he told me what it meant.

> I did not know,
> I did not know,
> I did not know,
> But now I know.

It took me going to Cuba to finally understand him.

I dug through Jack's war bag, found his Bible, and put it in my pack. When I stood up I nearly toppled over. I stumbled back up the hill, my head full of scorpions, my belly full of lizards. When I reached the top I dropped to the ground heaving my guts.

"Bully!" Roosevelt roared as he slapped a sergeant on the shoulder.

When I woke up the war was over. We were sailing home.

CHAPTER 27 August 1914

I suppose that war always does bring out
what is highest and lowest in human nature.

—THEODORE ROOSEVELT, *Theodore Roosevelt, an Autobiography*

TWO WEEKS LATER WE LANDED at Montauk, New York. I spent a month there recovering from the fever. Never completely got over it. Still get the shakes sometimes.

Colonel Roosevelt came around the infirmary to see the boys. He shook my hand and thanked me for helping win the war. We talked about the fight at Kettle Hill. He said it was the best day of his life.

Don't know what happened to Jack. When I got out of the infirmary I tried to find where the bodies were buried. No one seemed to know. I heard later that Colonel Roosevelt wanted to bring the boys home. Some were buried in graveyards around the country but the rest were left in Cuba. Don't believe Jack ever made it to Montana. Wished I could of done something about that.

Roosevelt didn't know how right he was when he called us Rough Riders. Times were rough for all of us. We were heroes when we came home, but a good many of us were dead from the fever within a few years.

I've thought a lot about the folks I've knowed over the years. Amigos, outlaws, soldiers, Indians. Colonel Roosevelt's the most famous. New

Mexico has a county named for him. Can you imagine? Like Lincoln County named after Ole Abe. The Colonel's one hell of a fighter. He has grit. Never flinched in Cuba. Never asked of his men what he wouldn't do hisself.

I've knowed other famous fighters. Heard the other day that Jim Younger killed hisself. Last time I saw Frank James he was selling shoes in Dallas. The best folks I've knowed didn't make names for theirselves. Folks like Paulita and María. María put fresh flowers on the mantle every day. There's a woman for you. Wish I knew what happened to her. Truth is I feel worser about her than I do about Paulita. It ain't right but it's how I feel. I should of come back earlier. For her and Paulita.

I've been powerful fortunate in my compadres too. Fred Waite, Kid Antrim, Jack Davis. Dick Brewer and John Tunstall. Buck and Maddie. Brother Jude—the raven I mean. And Mangel. Lord, I miss him every waking day. The best of them though was Brother Charles. Carlos to you, but he'll always be Brother Charles to me. He taught me the most. Most of my amigos saved my life one time or another. He saved my soul.

A Great War's cutting up Europe. Bigger than anything we've seen. The Lincoln County War was a pissant war but it was a great war to me. Cuba? That was real war, even if it lasted only a few weeks. You were in the Apache War. It lasted—what?—quarter of a century? That's longer than any war I've heard of. Here anyway. In the old country they had one lasted a hundred years. I can't comprehend that.

The paper says this one'll be bigger than the War between the States. Maybe the biggest ever. How generals keep up with wars like that I'll never figure. Moving men around like they know what they're doing. Hell, we didn't know what we were doing in the Lincoln County War when we knew the territory and all the fighters.

They say folks in London and Paris took to the streets cheering when war broke out. Poor dumb bastards. When it's over there'll be little left to cheer about. Only widows, orphans, and busted soldiers. Not heroes. Survivors.

Glory stories are bull anyway. Patriotic lies is more like it. But what glorious lies. For most of the boys it'll be hell. For a few it'll be a hell of a ride. It was for me. I loved everything about it. I never felt so—I don't know—noble?

I'd of hated war when I was in the thick of it if I hadn't loved it so much. The fear made my senses sharp as cactus spines. By the time I learned to hate it my warring days were done.

I've read a lot about war. Don't figure much good ever comes of it. Not enough to counter the carnage. I read somewhere that after Napoleon lost his empire at Waterloo, grave robbers stole teeth from the dead and sold the bones for fertilizer. Fifty thousand boys died so Tommies could have new teeth and brewers could have more barley. That there's your profits of war.

Every war I've ever knowed was based on a lie. Lies about John Tunstall caused the Lincoln County War. Lies about you caused the Apache War. Colonel Roosevelt asked us to remember the *Maine*, like the ship was the cause of it all. Hell, they still don't know why that damn ship went down. Three hundred boys died in the explosion but truth was the real casualty. I reckon it always is.

There'll be wars as long as there're folks to fight them. It's who we are. Only the dead ever see the end of it. I realized that with Carlos. He knew we were all brothers and shouldn't be killing each other. He tried to tell me but I didn't understand him. Not till Cuba. Still, after the massacre at the monastery he was ready to fight. He might of been there killing Comanches if Moze hadn't done him in. In the end I was grateful for Moze. Reckon Carlos was too.

That's it. Story's done. You're the only one I've ever told it to. Didn't expect I'd be so long-winded. There're still a couple of drafts of rotgut left. You take one, I'll take one, then let's get some supper. It's on me.

You know, I never believed that story about Tom Horn, why they hanged him. Can't believe he killed that boy. Wasn't like him. You and him were friends. Maybe you can tell me over supper what really happened.